*Tristram Shandy*

**Open Guides to Literature**

Series Editor: Graham Martin (Professor of Literature, The Open University)

*Titles in the Series*

Angus Calder: Byron
Jenni Calder: *Animal Farm* and *1984*
Walford Davies: Dylan Thomas
Roger Day: Larkin
Peter Faulkner: Yeats
P. N. Furbank: Pound
Brean Hammond: *Gulliver's Travels*
Graham Holderness: *Hamlet*
Graham Holderness: *Women in Love*
Graham Holderness: *Wuthering Heights*
Jeannette King: *Jane Eyre*
Graham Martin: *Great Expectations*
David B. Pirie: Shelley
Jeremy Tambling: What is Literary Language?
Dennis Walder: Ted Hughes
Roderick Watson: MacDiarmid
Ruth Whittaker: *Tristram Shandy*

Portrait of Laurence Sterne by an unknown artist.
(Courtesy of the National Portrait Gallery)

RUTH WHITTAKER

# *Tristram Shandy*

Open University Press
*Milton Keynes · Philadelphia*

Open University Press
Open University Educational Enterprises Limited
12 Cofferidge Close
Stony Stratford
Milton Keynes MK11 1BY

and

242 Cherry Street
Philadelphia, PA 19106, USA

First Published 1988

Copyright © Ruth Whittaker 1988

All rights reserved. No part of this publication may be reproduced, stored in a retrieval system or transmitted in any form or by any means, without written permission from the publisher.

**British Library Cataloguing in Publication Data**

Whittaker, Ruth
   Tristram Shandy.—(Open guides to literature).
   1. Fiction in English. Sterne, Laurence, 1713–1768. Tristram Shandy—Critical studies
   I. Title
   823'.6

ISBN 0-335-15264-3
ISBN 0-335-15263-5 Pbk

**Library of Congress Cataloging-in-Publication Data**

Whittaker, Ruth
   The life and opinions of Tristram Shandy.

   (Open guides to literature)
   Includes index.
   1. Sterne, Laurence, 1713–1768. Life and opinions of Tristram Shandy, gentleman.
I. Title.   II. Series.
PR3714.T73W4   1988     823'.6     88-19654
ISBN 0-335-15264-3
ISBN 0-335-15263-5 (pbk.)


Typeset by Rowland Phototypesetting Limited
Bury St Edmunds, Suffolk
Printed in Great Britain by
J. W. Arrowsmith Limited, Bristol

*For my godchildren
Elizabeth Andrews, Catherine Gillham
and Edmund Searle*

# Contents

| | |
|---|---|
| *Series Editor's Preface* | x |
| *Acknowledgements* | xii |
| 1  Introduction | 1 |
| 2  Contextual | 9 |
| 3  Sentiment, Sexuality and the Reader's Role | 22 |
| 4  Characterization | 41 |
| 5  Reflexive | 59 |
| 6  Time | 75 |
| *Notes* | 91 |
| *Suggestions for Further Reading* | 95 |
| *Index* | 99 |

# Series Editor's Preface

The intention of this series is to provide short introductory books about major writers, texts, and literary concepts for students of courses in Higher Education which substantially or wholly involve the study of Literature.

The series adopts a pedagogic approach and style similar to that of Open University material for Literature courses. *Open Guides* aim to inculcate the reading 'skills' which many introductory books in the field tend, mistakenly, to assume that the reader already possesses. They are, in this sense, 'teacherly' texts, planned and written in a manner which will develop in the reader the confidence to undertake further independent study of the topic. They are 'open' in two senses. First, they offer a three-way tutorial exchange between the writer of the *Guide*, the text or texts in question, and the reader. They invite readers to join in an exploratory discussion of texts, concentrating on their key aspects and on the main problems which readers, coming to the texts for the first time, are likely to encounter. The flow of a *Guide* 'discourse' is established by putting questions for the reader to follow up in a tentative and searching spirit, guided by the writer's comments, but not dominated by an over-arching and single-mindedly-pursued argument or evaluation, which itself requires to be 'read'.

*Guides* are also 'open' in a second sense. They assume that literary texts are 'plural', that there is no end to interpretation, and that it is for the reader to undertake the pleasurable task of discovering meaning and value in such texts. *Guides* seek to provide, in compact form, such relevant biographical, historical and cultural information as bears upon the reading of the text, and they point the reader to a selection of the best available critical discussions of it. They are not in themselves concerned to propose, or to counter, particular readings of the texts, but rather to put *Guide* readers in a position to do that for themselves. Experienced travellers learn to dispense with guides, and so it should be for readers of this series.

## Series Editor's Preface

This *Open Guide* to *Tristram Shandy* is best studied in conjunction with *Laurence Sterne: The Life and Opinions of Tristram Shandy*, edited by Graham Petrie, in the Penguin Classics edition (Penguin Books, 1967). Page references in the *Guide* are to this edition.

**Graham Martin**

# *Acknowledgements*

I should like to thank Kenneth and Julia Monkman for permission to reproduce the 'logo' of the Laurence Sterne Trust, the engraving of Shandy Hall on page 13. I am extremely grateful to Graham Martin for his invaluable advice, and for his most helpful editing. Without the companionship of Ernest Searle and the loving support of my husband, David Whittaker, this book would not have been completed. To them, my thanks.

# 1. Introduction

*Tristram Shandy* is one of the most extraordinary novels in English literature. It is very long, and very little seems to happen in the course of it, and yet it is possible for us to become intensely involved with the fates of its characters. It is extremely funny, with much of its humour at the reader's cost. It is also, paradoxically, a highly serious novel, debating the problems of artistic representation and the difficulties of conveying truth through the medium of fiction. I think its attraction lies in the way that these elements are interwoven, so that our interest in the characters may be suspended, but not diminished, by an authorial discussion of how best to represent them; an explanation of the techniques of fiction may be shot through with jokes and puns; humour may undermine a scene of pathos. It is a kaleidoscopic novel: rich and multicoloured, with many complicated and beautiful patterns.

It is a novel which has attracted a great deal of critical debate, but in this *Guide* I am going to concentrate on those aspects of it which are appropriate to a first reading, i.e. the themes of *Tristram Shandy*, the characterization, Sterne's interest in the fictional representation of reality, and his impatience with the limitations of language. *Tristram Shandy* was first published in instalments, and I think it's still best read intermittently, a few chapters at a time. Don't be put off by the number of learned allusions and Latin phrases scattered throughout the novel. Many of Sterne's esoteric references are invented, or offered satirically, so you needn't feel obliged to look up every one. I will begin in this chapter by looking only at the first two volumes of *Tristram Shandy*. From Chapter 3 onwards I will assume that you have completed your first reading of the whole novel.

**Please now read Chapter 1 (pp. 35–6).**

Even allowing for the fact that *Tristram Shandy* was written over two hundred years ago, it may strike you on first reading as a very strange, unconventional novel. Part of this strangeness has to do with Sterne's prose style, and it would be useful to look at this first of all.

After reading the chapter, make a note of whatever strikes you as distinctive about Sterne's prose.

## DISCUSSION

You may have included 'elaborate' or 'convoluted' or 'rambling' in your notes on the style of this first chapter. It is certainly not clear and succinct: the sentences are long, loose and discursive, and contain several subordinate clauses. The first sentence, for example, is fourteen lines long; the second, fifteen. The clauses are separated by commas, semicolons, colons, and innumerable dashes of varying length to indicate pauses. The punctuation seems almost arbitrary. You will notice that in the first sentence the subject matter moves from the narrator's parents to the far-reaching effects of the conditions of conception, almost in a crescendo from 'body' to 'mind' to 'the fortunes of his whole house'. Both the first and second sentences have a cumulative effect, with Sterne piling clause upon clause, so that by the end of a sentence it is sometimes difficult for the reader to remember the main subject of it. For example, in the second sentence 'their' and 'them' and 'they' refer back to the 'animal spirits', but it needs a pause to grasp this. It's as if Sterne is writing as he thinks, following the wanderings of his mind, rather than working out what he wants to say beforehand and tailoring his prose to fit his thought. I find the effect is initially disconcerting; it is simultaneously both formal and colloquial. The difficulty of the intricate syntax is complemented by words and phrases, probably archaic to a twentieth-century reader, such as 'begot', 'verily', 'humours', 'rational Being', 'cast of his mind' and 'animal spirits'.

Nevertheless the style has a conversational tone, which stems partly from the narrator's asides to the reader, in phrases such as 'Believe me, good folks' and 'you may take my word'. It also derives from Sterne's use of the dash, one of the hallmarks of his style. If you look carefully, you'll see that the length of each dash varies considerably, 'like skid marks where he has to brake or accelerate'.[1] Each one indicates a separation from the previous clause; they are not so abrupt as a full stop, or as brief as a comma, and the impression is of a fast, almost breathless, flow of ideas.

There is also much vivid imagery—'cluttering like hey-go-mad' —and its effect is impressionistic, almost surreal. Even as early as the first page of *Tristram Shandy* he is trying to describe a state of being that cannot be accommodated by literal, realistic language, but demands an elaborate metaphor which enacts the 'motions and activity' as well as describing it. Sterne does not make concessions to the reader in terms of simple language or careful explanations. The

## Introduction

last paragraph of dialogue between the narrator's parents is presented abruptly, with no helpful transitional sentence to alert us to a change of scene. And finally, the mention of 'the creation of the world' acts as an implicit metaphor for the creation of Sterne's fictional world. We, as readers, are in at the beginning, as it were, of the lives of the narrator—Tristram Shandy—and the novel, *The Life and Opinions of Tristram Shandy*.

So: this first chapter usefully introduces us to typical aspects of the novel. First, Sterne's habit of digressing: he takes a long time to get to the main point of the story; second, the meandering sentences which seem to be an unedited version of his thoughts; third, his use of words and phrases which would have been easily understood in the eighteenth century, but which may demand more thought from us; fourth, his asides to an imagined reader; and fifth, the reflexive nature of *Tristram Shandy*; that is to say, the way in which this novel reflects on the process of literary creativity. It is self-referential, a novel about the problems of writing a novel. These characteristics may not make for easy reading at first, but as you become familiar with them they will seem entirely appropriate to the leisurely pace of the novel.

\* \* \*

*Tristram Shandy* begins with the first person singular—'I'—which immediately introduces us to the narrator, although we don't actually learn his name until Chapter 4. It is important at the outset to understand the theoretical distinction between the author and the narrator. The author invents a narrator, the one who is telling the story. His views and tone need not necessarily correspond with those of the author, but often they do. As we'll see in Chapters 2 and 3 of the *Guide*, Sterne's own personality closely resembles that of his narrator, Tristram Shandy, and this sometimes makes it difficult, if not impossible, to differentiate between them. The difficulty is not so great in a novel where the author bears no resemblance to the narrator.

**Would you now reread Volume I, Chapter 1 and read on to the end of Chapter 6, in order to answer the following questions:**
1 How does the narrator build up a relationship with his readers?
2 What seems to be expected of us?

DISCUSSION

1 It seems to me that in these chapters the narrator uses three techniques to build up a relationship with his readers:

(a) He mentions his awareness of his potential readership. Such phrases as 'in which the reader is likely to see me' (Ch. 1) and 'I know there are readers in the world . . . who find themselves ill at ease . . .' (Ch. 4) include the reader in the process of writing. In other words, the narrator foregrounds the problem of holding the reader's attention, an aspect of writing that is not usually referred to by a conventional novelist.

(b) The narrator addresses his readers directly: 'Believe me, good folks', and 'You may take my word' (Ch. 1); 'You have all, I dare say, heard of the animal spirits' (Ch. 4). The inclusive 'you' draws us into a direct relationship with the narrator. These confidential asides give a kind of intimacy to the prose, and allow Sterne to write about sexuality, for example, as if his narrator were talking with one person, rather than writing for a wide readership.

(c) He invents an imaginary but specific listener, sometimes a man, sometimes a woman, and addresses the narrative especially to that person. For instance, in Chapter 2 the reader is called 'dear Sir'. In Chapter 4 there is suddenly a female listener, to whom the narrator refers as 'Madam'. In Chapter 6 the reader is again called 'Sir' and also 'my dear friend and companion.' The narrator not only invents listeners/readers, but also gives them dialogue. At the end of Chapters 1 and 4, it is the supposed listener who asks the leading questions about Walter Shandy, enabling the narrator to give his oblique and witty answers.

2  Those oblique answers remind us that as readers, Sterne expects a high level of participation from us. The narrator makes assumptions (sometimes tinged with irony) about an educated readership: 'You have all, I dare say, heard of the animal spirits . . .'. He invites our involvement in the plot by giving us important information obscurely, and expecting us to work hard to get to grips with what is actually being said. You will have noticed that in Chapter 1 there is a great deal of opinion and not much action, and it may not have been easy on a first reading to understand what actually takes place. This is because Sterne doesn't actually *tell* us. If you understood that this first chapter is about interrupted sexual intercourse, you did so by a process of deduction. In the last line of Chapter 1 Sterne has his narrator bring in an imaginary listener, who conveniently asks 'Pray what was your father saying?'. 'Nothing' is the answer, and so we are left to infer what he was *doing*. We do this by remembering the first paragraph where the narrator wishes his parents 'had minded what they were about when they begot me'.

Chapter 6 is explicitly about the relationship between the narrator and the reader. This relationship is built up with delicacy

# Introduction

and tact. The narrator knows that he is making considerable demands on the reader, and so invites both friendship and tolerance. This chapter is important, because here Sterne recognizes the possible impatience of a reader concerned with getting on with the story, unhindered by digressions. But we are told 'You must have a little patience' and we are asked, disarmingly, for our forebearance and co-operation: '... my dear friend and companion, if you should think somewhat sparing of my narrative on my first setting out, bear with me,—and let me go on, and tell my story my own way.' Sterne is extremely interested in his unknown readers, and we become, in a sense, characters in his novel, to be manipulated just as they are. He constantly teases us, and leads us into traps. For example, later in Volume I the narrator is talking about a friendship with a woman: 'Surely, Madam, a friendship between the two sexes may subsist, and be supported without—'. At this point an apparently shocked female listener is made to interject 'Fy! Mr Shandy: ——' The narrator goes on triumphantly: 'Without any thing, Madam, but that tender and delicious sentiment, which ever mixes in friendship, where there is a difference of sex.' (I, 18, p. 76) Here Sterne is exploiting the impure mind of the reader whom he has led on to imagine the worst, and then adroitly extricated himself from fulfilling those expectations. Thus the implicit accusation of indecency rebounds from Sterne to his reader, with the narrator expressing mock surprise at the reader's impurity. Much of the humour in *Tristram Shandy*, particularly the sexual humour, relies upon our understanding of the *double entendre*, and the reader is subjected to the Catch-22 implicit in all such jokes: to the pure all things are pure, therefore if you understand the joke you shouldn't be shocked by it. Sterne is attacking not purity, but prudery and hypocrisy.

**In order to begin to appreciate the diversity of this novel, would you now attempt to disentangle the central story of the first six chapters from the subsidiary material. List the events you think constitute the main thread of the novel, and then list the other topics Sterne offers us.**

DISCUSSION

I have isolated as central Tristram's interrupted conception and the mention of his birth (although this is not actually completed until Volume III). Everything else seems to me to be opinion, philosophy, explanation of literary technique and exhortations to the reader. *Tristram Shandy* is a leisurely book in the sense that we are asked to ruminate, to become involved in the narrator's emotions and speculations. His range of topics is extremely wide. For example, he includes in the first six chapters a theory that the outcome of a person's life is very largely dependent on the conditions of his or her conception; a description of the Homunculus as an entire human being, and the perils of his (in this case, Tristram's) journey to the womb; references to readers' expectations, and literary mentors such as Montaigne and Horace; John Locke's theory of the association of ideas; reflections on astrology; and an appeal to the reader for patience.

This wide variety of subject matter alerts us to one of the recurrent themes of this novel, which is about the difficulty of selection. This, of course, is an essential task of any novelist, and the reader's attention is not usually drawn to it. Sterne, however, revels in this problem and refuses to succumb to it. He introduces numerous digressions which have already subverted the story line after only a few pages of the novel. His love of digression is related to his interest in John Locke and the association of ideas, whereby disparate thoughts and ideas are linked together without any logical or causal connections. We will look at this issue later—pp. 16–18. In Chapter 4 Sterne makes it clear that he does not intend to confine himself to the literary rules of Horace, 'nor to any man's rules that ever lived' (p. 38). This reflexive activity, this drawing attention to the medium, is not the procedure of a conventional realist writer. He or she normally wants the reader to become lost in the story, to believe in the characters, and to turn the pages in suspense to find out what is going to happen. And all this as if the novel's content were real, not imaginary. Coleridge called our ability to accept art as reality (albeit only temporarily) a 'willing suspension of disbelief'[2] and in plays or novels which adopt a 'realist' convention we accede to this 'suspension' quite happily. But Sterne does not allow us to do this in *Tristram Shandy*. In reading it, we partly succumb to the persuasion of the narrator—we 'believe' in the story—and simultaneously experience a feeling of resistance to it. This resistance is, paradoxically, strengthened by the narrator, who constantly draws our attention to the elusive and approximate nature of the medium (words) and the inadequacy of realist conventions to convey reality.

**Would you now read to the end of Volume I. When you have done so, reread Chapters 14 and 22, which are on the subject of digression. What is the narrator's defence of digression?**

DISCUSSION

In Chapter 14 the narrator says that digression is inevitable for a writer, 'For, if he is a man of the least spirit he will have fifty

## Introduction

deviations from a straight line to make with this or that party as he goes along, which he can no ways avoid'. (p. 64) But he acknowledges the difficulties that digressions cause to the progress of his chronicle, and the possibility of infinite regression: 'I declare I have been at it these six weeks, making all the speed I possibly could,—and am not yet born'. In Chapter 22 the defence is more elaborate. The narrator says that although he does digress, he simultaneously attends to the progression of the novel's plot. Yet ironically, the example he gives of the 'main business' of the novel is his description of Uncle Toby's character.

> I was just going, for example, to have given you the great outlines of my uncle Toby's most whimsical character;—when my aunt Dinah and the coachman came across us, and led us a vagary some millions of miles into the very heart of the planetary system: Notwithstanding all this you perceive that the drawing of my uncle Toby's character went on gently all the time . . . (p. 94)

Later in the chapter the narrator reverts to the paradoxical proposition that the digressions are in fact the essence of *Tristram Shandy*: 'Digressions, incontestably, are the sunshine;—they are the life, the soul of reading;—take them out of this book for instance,—you might as well take the book along with them;' (p. 95). So by this time any lingering expectations of *Tristram Shandy* as a conventional sequential narrative should be abandoned. These are expectations relevant to realist art which can simplify or impose a sense-making pattern on the seeming chaos of ordinary life. But Sterne is concerned with trying to convey the amazing complexity of everyday living, and the ways in which, for example, our words and actions are influenced by unconscious and irrational motives. Thus for him his material needs to be reflected through a non-sequential narrative, since in real life our thought-processes are not linear. Digression, in fact, is one of Sterne's narrative devices for conveying this complexity, so that an account of his hero's birth includes the history of the mid-wife, the history and character of the clergyman who paid the fee for the mid-wife's licence (a digression of nearly twenty pages), and even a section about his mother's marriage settlement relating to childbirth, his father's character and political theories, theological arguments about baptism and the character of his Uncle Toby.

A further way of attempting to transcend the verbal, linear momentum of the normal narrative form is the use of visual effects. **Would you now look through Volume I, and list the different typographical variations from the printed word that you would not usually find in a novel. What is the purpose of each kind of device? What do you think Sterne is trying to convey on pages 61 and 62 (Ch. 12)?**

## DISCUSSION

In Volume I Sterne uses dashes to indicate pauses of varying lengths, and also to avoid blasphemy ('Good G—!') or to preserve a kind of anonymity (In the county of——'). He uses italics and capital letters in the middle of the text for emphasis and for foreign phrases. Asterisks on pp. 58, 60 and 79 are used to avoid naming people and places, although later in the novel they frequently mask bawdy or obscenity. We are given a pleasing visual pun on p. 38 (Ch. 4) when the narrator says

──────────────── Shut the door ────────────────

The line across the page suggests a sense of privacy, of enclosure. The lines drawn around ⌐Alas poor YORICK!¬ (p. 60) symbolize his tombstone, and the black pages underline the narrator's sorrow at his death. The legal nature of Mrs Shandy's marriage settlement is emphasized by the Gothic lettering, and finally, at the end of Volume I we are given a blank page to indicate that the narrator has torn a page out of the book that he is writing. (Presumably a ragged, torn edge would have suited Sterne better, but even he had to submit to the technical limitations of book production!)

The black pages 61 and 62 are the most striking of Sterne's typographical exploitations in Volume I. Ordinary illustrations in novels are somewhat different: they may enhance the text, but they are not intended to replace it. These black pages are *instead* of words. They convey sorrow and deep mourning in a much more immediate way than if we simply read about them. We may feel that Sterne is cheating a bit because we come to a novel with the expectation that words alone are the novelist's medium, and that he or she will strive to make them adequate for their purpose. In a realistic novel, if words are deemed to fall short of their task, the narrator usually employs clichés such as 'mere words could not express her feelings'. Sterne acknowledges this dilemma, but he then goes one step further, breaks the rules, and does something about it. The shock of the black pages bypasses our intellect and engages our emotions. It is, of course, a joke at the expense of the reader. We expect words in a book, and suddenly we are given no words. How do we cope with the abrupt appearance of these black pages? Do we shed a tear for Yorick, or meditate on death for the amount of time it would have taken us to read the page if it were readable? The pages work very effectively to vary the pace of our response to the earlier narrative. They force on us a pause, which can both symbolize the end of Yorick's life, and give us time to reflect on endings, death, darkness and sorrow, to use the pages as a *memento mori*.

By using black pages instead of words, Sterne conveys very strongly the idea that words are often totally inadequate to express deep emotion, and indeed that it may not always be appropriate to make the attempt to do so through this medium. The fact that a sorrow may lie too deep for words is made very literal by Sterne's rejection of them. He was particularly interested in the challenge of effective communication, and shared John Locke's views about the problematic nature of words for that purpose. The black pages clearly convey Sterne's distrust of words. His scepticism about them, while he remains simultaneously dependent upon them for his novel, is a paradox to which he reverts continually throughout *Tristram Shandy*.

In this first chapter of the *Guide* we have looked at the most striking features of *Tristram Shandy* for the first time reader: Sterne's fondness for digression and his appropriately discursive style; the relationship of the narrator with his readers, and the effects of typographical oddities on the printed page. These aspects will be looked at in more detail in the course of this *Guide*. The next chapter is about Sterne's background and the influences on his work. Meanwhile, here is Sterne's own description of 'Shandeism', the motivating spirit of the novel:

> True Shandeism, think what you will against it, opens the heart and lungs, and like all those affections which partake of its nature, it forces the blood and other vital fluids of the body to run freely through its channels, and makes the wheel of life run long and cheerfully round.   (IV, 32, p. 333)

# 2. Contextual

In order to begin to appreciate a work of literature, it's often helpful to know something about the author, and about the cultural climate in which he or she worked. In this Chapter I shall look briefly at Sterne's life and character, and the influences on *Tristram Shandy*. I shall also set the novel in its eighteenth-century context, to see how it both reflects and deviates from the literary conventions of that time.

Laurence Sterne was born at Clonmel in Southern Ireland on 24 November, 1713. His great-grandfather was Richard Sterne, Master of Jesus College, Cambridge, and subsequently Archbishop of York. His father Roger was an impoverished member of the family, a humble ensign who fought in the Flanders wars under Marlborough. In 1711, aged nineteen, he married Agnes, the widowed daughter of an army sutler, a supplier of provisions to the troops. This marriage was undoubtedly a foolish one in social and economic terms. Roger's two brothers both married heiresses, and lived in Yorkshire. But Roger's army life was peripatetic, and his wife either stayed with relations or followed her husband from camp to camp. Until the age of ten Laurence Sterne's childhood was spent between Ireland and England, travelling from one place to the other according to the itinerary of his father's regiment. There was no continuity, however, no joyful returning to familiar scenes. Although the first seventeen months of Sterne's life were spent in Yorkshire, his mother was not befriended by the Sterne family, and on subsequent visits to England she lodged variously at Liverpool, Plymouth, Bath and the Isle of Wight.

When he was six years old, Sterne 'learned to write &c'[1]. His teacher may have been a Lieutenant Lefever, the name he uses later in *Tristram Shandy* for the story of the soldier and his son.[2] What is certain is that when he was ten, Laurence was sent to school in England, near Halifax, and stayed there until he was eighteen. He never returned to his parents or to Ireland. Indeed, he was not to see his father again, because Roger Sterne died in Jamaica with his regiment, in 1731. We can only imagine the effect of those eight years at boarding school on Laurence Sterne. It is possible that he felt very lonely and abandoned. He was near to his relatives, but there is no evidence of any close ties with them. Neither his father nor his wealthy Yorkshire uncle paid his school fees, and Sterne himself was presented with a bill from the school when he obtained his first job as a clergyman. The schoolmaster he was most influenced by was called Nathan Sharpe, and in his memoirs Sterne gives us one anecdote about his schooldays. The master had

> had the cieling [sic] of the school-room new white-washed—the ladder remained there—I one unlucky day mounted it, and wrote with a brush in large capital letters, LAU. STERNE, for which the usher severely whipped me. My master was very much hurt at this, and said, before me, that never should that name be effaced, for I was a boy of genius, and he was sure I should come to preferment—this expression made me forget the stripes I had received.[3]

There is no record of Sterne's life between leaving school in 1731 and going to Cambridge in 1733. In 1732 his uncle Richard died, leaving substantial estates and money in his will, but nothing to his nephew Laurence. His surviving uncle Jacques refused to help him, and Sterne felt this keenly. In later years he expresses his gratitude to his cousin Richard 'to whose Protection *then*, I Cheifly owe What I now am.'[4] So: a shifting, unsettled childhood, deprived of parental contact from the age of ten, and made very aware of his status as a poor relation. Perhaps as a result Sterne seemed incapable of making close and lasting relationships. It is also unsurprising that money was important to him, and that his delight at the success of *Tristram Shandy* was as much for the financial security as for the fame it brought him.

In 1733, aged nearly twenty, Sterne went up to Jesus College, Cambridge. After a year, he was awarded one of the scholarships founded by his great-grandfather, which together with the £30 a year from his cousin Richard, enabled him to survive. Sterne would have continued his study of the classics, begun at school. Philosophy was taught: Descartes, Locke and Newton. Other writers who clearly influenced him, such as Shakespeare, Cervantes, Rabelais, Swift and Pope he would have read for pleasure and not as part of the undergraduate curriculum. Supervision was lax, and it was possible to graduate without having done much work. At Cambridge he suffered the first symptoms of tuberculosis, which plagued him intermittently for the rest of his life, and which eventually killed him. It's probable that Sterne went to Cambridge on the understanding that he would enter the church, and two months after taking his BA in 1737 he was ordained a deacon and given a curacy at St Ives in Huntingdonshire. He spent a year there before going back to Yorkshire, briefly working as a curate and then, after being ordained a priest, as vicar of Sutton, eight miles north of York.

Sterne remained vicar of Sutton for the next twenty years, although for some of that time he lodged in York and engaged a curate to carry out day-to-day duties in the parish. While living in the city Sterne met numerous attractive women, and he gained a reputation as someone who 'delighted in debauchery'.[5] It was in York that he met Elizabeth Lumley, the daughter of a clergyman, who had a small inheritance from her parents. They married in 1741, and had one child who survived to adulthood, Lydia. An earlier daughter lived only for one day, and Elizabeth had at least one miscarriage, probably more. Their marriage was not a success. It would seem that Elizabeth was not easy to live with. A cousin wrote of her:

> M^rs Sterne is a Woman of great integrity and has many virtues, but they stand like quills upon the fretfull porcupine, ready to go forth in

sharp arrows on y^e least supposed offence; she w^d not do a wrong thing, but she does right things in a very unpleasing manner, & the only way to avoid a quarrel with her is to keep a due distance. I have not seen M^rs Sterne since I was a girl in hanging sleeves, but I know her character well.[6]

Relations with his wife were not helped by Sterne's mother, Agnes, and his younger sister Catherine, who came to England from Ireland in 1741 after hearing exaggerated reports of Elizabeth's wealth. Agnes had visited her son in England only once in the previous eighteen years, and Laurence had no love for her. He and Elizabeth were constantly harassed by her demands for money, and the sad and bitter dispute lasted until Agnes' death in 1759. But as well as financial difficulties, the Sternes' marriage was strained to breaking point by Laurence's frequent infidelities. Sterne slept with girls in York procured for him by his man-servant, and had affairs with visiting actresses. There is also a story that his wife once caught him in bed with a maid. From the beginning of the 1750s, Sterne and his wife increasingly led separate lives, and in about 1759 Elizabeth had a severe nervous breakdown.

During his years at Sutton, Sterne dabbled in farming and in politics, and some of his earliest published writings were for the Whig newspaper the *York Gazetteer*, founded by his uncle Jacques. In 1759 he wrote a pamphlet called *A Political Romance*, a satire about a diocesan quarrel, soon suppressed. During 1759 Sterne was also writing *Tristram Shandy*, and in May he offered the first volume to a London publisher, Robert Dodsley for £50. Dodsley rejected it at first, saying that it was economically too risky to publish it. Sterne did some rewriting, and made the satire less personal and local. In October of the same year he wrote again to Dodsley saying that he planned to publish two volumes of the novel in York at his own expense. This was a shrewd move, and Dodsley agreed to take half the copies to try to sell in London. Late in December 1759 *Tristram Shandy* was published in York and sold two hundred copies in two days. It was reviewed in *The Monthly Review*, a London periodical, and Dodsley swiftly sold all the copies he had taken. On 4 March, 1760, Sterne arrived in London, and on 8 March made a formal agreement with James Dodsley, Robert's brother. He sold the copyright of the first four volumes of *Tristram Shandy* for £630 and agreed to write a new volume every year. This sum was later amended, so that Sterne received a total of £830 in return for the first four volumes plus a volume of Sterne's sermons which he published under the pseudonym Yorick. This was almost three times Sterne's annual income as a clergyman, and he was immensely excited about it. Dodsley immediately published a second edition, with a frontis-

1   Engraving of Shandy Hall, Coxwold

piece by Hogarth, and a dedication to Pitt, which Sterne had composed while in London. The novel caused a great stir, and Sterne became a celebrity almost overnight. His life changed thereafter. In 1760 Lord Fauconberg offered him the living of Coxwold, in Yorkshire. He accepted, calling it 'a sweet retirement in comparison of Sutton'.[7]

Sterne had been consumptive for most of his life (as was his wife) and he was now able to travel to warmer climates. He spent a year in Toulouse, where he was joined by his wife and daughter. Later he travelled in both France and Italy, and from this experience he wrote *A Sentimental Journey*, which was published in 1768. In 1766 he met and fell in love with Eliza Draper, a young woman of twenty-two, who had been married to an older man in India since she was fourteen. Sterne knew her for only two months before she returned to India, but he wrote intensely romantic letters to her, which were published in 1773. His *Journal to Eliza* wasn't published until 1904.

On 18 March, 1768, Sterne's weak constitution finally succumbed to pleurisy, and he died in London, aged fifty-four. He was buried in Paddington, which at that time was open country, and neither his widow nor daughter (who were in France) attended his funeral. There is, however, a wonderful Shandean postscript to his story. Some time after his death, a rumour arose that Sterne's newly-buried body had been taken by body-snatchers, and used for an anatomy lecture at Cambridge. Someone was thought to have recognized him, and he was hastily reburied in Paddington. In 1968 the Laurence Sterne Trust exhumed a grave thought to be that of Sterne, and found several bones and skulls, one of which had had the top sawn off. This would have been the result either of a postmortem or an anatomical dissection, and as postmortems in the eighteenth century were extremely rare, this substantiated the gruesome story of Sterne's remains. The skull was measured by a Harley Street surgeon,

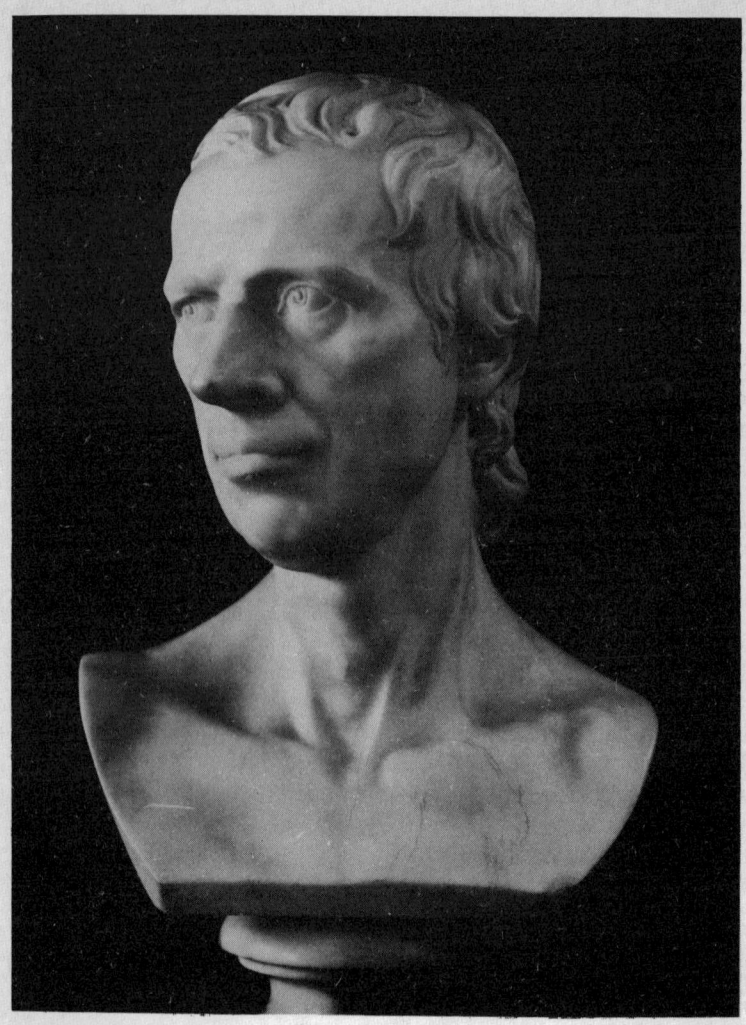

2   Profile of J. Nollekens' bust of Laurence Sterne (Courtesy of the National Portrait Gallery)

and compared with a bust of Sterne made in his lifetime by a famous sculptor called Joseph Nollekens. Sterne's head was unusually small for his height, and the measurements of his skull matched perfectly. It was reburied in Coxwold churchyard on 8 June, 1969. I can't help thinking how greatly Sterne himself would have enjoyed this macabre affair; restless to the end, and restless even after death.

\* \* \*

Let us now look at some of the influences on Sterne which greatly affected his writing of *Tristram Shandy*. Sterne was influenced by numerous earlier writers, even though *Tristram Shandy* is so strikingly original. *Don Quixote*, the novel written by Cervantes (1547–1616) in the early seventeenth century, satirizing the chivalric tradition, was published in an English translation in 1719. Sterne loved *Don Quixote*, and compares Parson Yorick with Cervantes' creation. Part of his comic method clearly derives from Cervantes. He wrote in a letter: 'I am perswaded that the happiness of the Cervantic humour arises from . . . describing silly and trifling Events, with the Circumstantial Pomp of great Ones'.[8] Another great comic writer to whom he is indebted is Rabelais (c. 1494–c. 1553), whose works were published in English between 1653 and 1694. He probably read Rabelais at Cambridge, and the library at Skelton Castle (the home of his friend John Hall-Stevenson) was stocked with the works of Rabelais and other salacious literature. *Tristram Shandy* owes a great deal to *Gargantua* and *Pantagruel*, and before *Tristram Shandy* Sterne had written a 'Fragment in the Manner of Rabelais', which was not published until 1775, after his death. The influence of Rabelais shows not only in the bawdy jokes and *double-entendres* of *Tristram Shandy*, but also in its style. Encouraged by his example, Sterne uses language with wild extravagance, and with a total disregard for moderation or decorum. The excess, the breathless and anarchic quality of *Tristram Shandy* is highly Rabelaisian, an aspect of Sterne's work that was heavily criticized in the nineteenth century.

Swift's satire *A Tale of a Tub* (1704) greatly impressed Sterne, and both the suppressed work *A Political Romance* and *Tristram Shandy* owe much to Swift. In the latter Sterne imitates Swift's parodies of literary conventions—dedications, prefaces and introductions. Nevertheless, their satire is very different. Sterne is gentle and humorous. He follows his words, as it were, to see where they will take him, fuelled by a sense of absurdity rather than anger.

A writer who provided a rich source for *Tristram Shandy* was Robert Burton (1577–1640), another clergyman, who was the author of *The Anatomy of Melancholy* (1621). Burton himself was a great plagiarist, and at the beginning of Volume VII of *Tristram Shandy* Sterne copies him shamelessly.[9] Burton is prodigal with words. Like Rabelais he indulges in catalogues, and long lists of synonyms, a practice copied by Sterne. But what is also interesting is that the unity of *The Anatomy of Melancholy* is achieved by the persona of the narrator, who intervenes frequently in the text, and who establishes a chatty relationship with his reader. Similarly, Montaigne (1533–92), another strong influence on Sterne, emerges as a distinct character in his *Essays*. In them he gives a running commentary on the process of writing, and this reflexivity is a significant element of *Tristram Shandy*.[10]

Like Rabelais, Burton and Swift, Sterne was writing within what has been called the 'tradition of learned wit'.[11] This was the comic exploitation of medieval systems of knowledge from the viewpoint of the Enlightenment, so that certain themes, chiefly medical, legal and theological, are repeatedly satirised. Or, perhaps not so much satirised as juxtaposed with the human concerns and errors of everyday living. Thus, in *Tristram Shandy*, the vital process of conception is interrupted by a trivial question, with disastrous consequences; Tristram's birthplace provokes prodigious legal wrangles, and the question of baptism stimulates a lengthy theological argument. Sterne is very conscious of incongruities between theories and their application; systems and the individual.

It would be as easy as it is unnecessary (the footnotes do it for you) to make a long list of influences on Sterne; sources he pillaged, styles he copied. Sterne was a magpie, and *Tristram Shandy* is a complex construction, interwoven with stolen pieces of silk and feathers and jewels. The point is that Sterne's originality lies neither in his style, nor in his material, nor in the persona of his narrator, but in the way he achieves a kind of alchemy, whereby the mixture results in something both extraordinary and unique.

But certain influences we do need to consider in more detail, notably that of the English philosopher, John Locke (1632–1704). In 1690 he published his *Essay Concerning Human Understanding*, a work extensively influential during the eighteenth century. It elaborates a theory of knowledge now described as 'empiricist'. The fundamental thesis is that all knowledge is derived from experience through the medium of our senses:

> Let us then suppose the mind to be, as we say, white paper, void of all characters, without any ideas; how comes it to be furnished? Whence comes it by that vast store, which the busy and boundless fancy of man has painted on it with an almost endless variety? Whence has it all the materials of reason and knowledge? To this I answer, in one word, from experience: in that all our knowledge is founded, and from that it ultimately derives itself.[12]

According to this theory, there are no innate ideas, no 'essence' apart from a general idea deduced from verbal definitions. Locke makes a distinction between simple ideas, which are the data given by the perception of our senses, and complex ideas, which are formed by the mind operating upon these data. Sterne was immensely interested in Locke, and in *Tristram Shandy* he asks an imaginary literary critic:

> Pray Sir, in all the reading which you have ever read, did you ever read such a book as Locke's *Essay upon the Human Understanding*? —Don't answer me rashly—because many, I know, quote the book, who have not read it,—and many have read it who understand it not;—if either of these is your case, as I write to instruct, I will tell you in three words what the book is.—It is a history.—A history! of who? what? where? when? Don't hurry yourself.—It is a history-book, Sir, (which may possibly recommend it to the world) of what passes in a man's own mind... (II, 2, pp. 106–7)

Locke was centrally concerned about the difficulty of communication. He did not claim that words were an adequate representation of reality, but that if they are the only means of conveying our perception of it, then it's very important that we have a consensus about the relationship of words with what they express. In other words, there needs to be a general agreement that certain words represent certain concepts. We all need to agree, for example, that the word 'green' is normally used to describe the colour of grass, or that a furry, feline quadruped may be represented by the word 'cat', if we are to communicate effectively with one another.

Another aspect of Locke's work which intrigued Sterne was what was called the 'association of ideas'. This is the irrational linking together of disparate thoughts, whereby one automatically conjures up the other. Locke writes:

> Ideas that in themselves are not all of kin, come to be so united in some men's minds, that it is very hard to separate them; they always keep in company, and the one no sooner at any time comes into the understanding, but its associate appears with it; and if they are more than two which are thus united, the whole gang, always inseparable, show themselves together.[13]

*Tristram Shandy* begins with a wonderful example of the association of ideas. You'll remember from Chapter 4 that Mr Shandy wound the house clock on the first Sunday of every month, and 'brought some other little family concernments to the same period, in order ... to get them all out of the way at one time ...' (I, 4). Tristram describes the effect of these two events on the mind of his mother:

> ... from an unhappy association of ideas, which have no connection in nature, so it fell out at length, that my poor mother could never hear the said clock wound up,——but the thoughts of some other things unavoidably popped into her head—& *vice versa*:——which strange combination of ideas, the sagacious Locke, who certainly understood the nature of these things better than most men, affirms to have produced more wry actions than all other sources of prejudice whatsoever. (I, 4, p. 39)

These inappropriate associations delight Sterne with their irrational and illogical nature. Thus, when Obadiah announces to the Shandys' maid Susannah that Tristram's brother has died,

> A green satin night-gown of my mother's, which had been twice scoured, was the first idea which Obadiah's exclamation brought into Susannah's head.—Well might Locke write a chapter upon the imperfections of words. (V, 7, p. 354)

The linking train of unconscious thought, which becomes omitted in the association of ideas, is later given to the reader. Susannah thinks that the death of Mrs Shandy's son will be the death of her, and then she, Susannah, will inherit her wardrobe of clothes, including the coveted green satin nightgown. During *Tristram Shandy* Sterne plays with the association of ideas, some of which run like leitmotifs throughout the novel. In some cases he actually generates the ideas in his readers' minds, and then evokes the association economically by referring to only one aspect of it. For example, having made great play on the subject of noses, in Volume III, Chapter 31, implying a *double entendre*, Sterne's use of the word 'nose' invariably conjures up other connotations thereafter.

Before leaving the question of influences on Sterne's work, we need to consider that of other eighteenth century novelists. Sterne's literary predecessors in England include Defoe (1660–1731), Swift (1667–1745), Richardson (1689–1761), Fielding (1707–54), Smollett (1721–71) and Johnson (1709–84). These eminent practitioners did not write from a consensus about the novel form, which indeed was being created during the eighteenth century in the shape that we know it today and there was a great deal of diversity between them. What they had in common, however, was their refusal to rely on traditional plots for their work. Earlier writers, such as Chaucer, Shakespeare and Milton took their plots from mythology, history or earlier literature. Defoe, Richardson and Fielding were some of the first writers in English literature to invent their own plots, in which the narrative is subordinated to the author's personal inclinations. This trend emphasizes the validity of the individual perception of the author, and a desire to move away from acceptance of universalized truths which could be sufficiently expressed in fable or allegory. It also stresses the importance of the particular over the general, and this movement in literature reflects the growing philosophical tendency towards individualization. Descartes had given immense importance to the thought processes within the consciousness of an individual, and Locke and Hume subsequently emphasized the significance of the individual's memory in the construction of a personal identity, i.e. the linking of a chain of causes and events which help us to understand what sort of people we are.

This growing interest in the individual and the particular is reflected in the emergence of what has come to be called 'realism'. Ian Watt has given us a useful description of the realistic convention as applied to the novel form when he says that Defoe and Richardson worked on the premise

> that the novel is a full and authentic report of human experience, and is therefore under an obligation to satisfy its reader with such details of the story as the individuality of the actors concerned, the particulars of the times and places of their actions, details which are presented through a more largely referential use of language than is common in other literary forms.[14]

The 'individuality' of the characters is emphasized by the titles of many eighteenth century novels, which were often simply the names of their protagonists, for example, *Robinson Crusoe* (1719), *Moll Flanders* (1722), *Pamela* (1740), *Clarissa* (1748), *Joseph Andrews* (1742), *Tom Jones* (1749). Their authors assume, too, that the reader will be interested in their doings, even though they are not mythical, historical or allegorical figures. Our interest in a character called Tristram Shandy is likely to be of a different order from our interest in allegorical characters called 'Hope' or 'Despair' or anonymous princely figures such as Musidorus and Pyrocles in Sidney's romance *Arcadia* (1581). Such names are so obviously allegorical that we do not expect life-like detail in order to convince us of their 'reality'. This is not to say that Sidney's readers did not identify with his courtly figures. But 'realist' characterisation addressed a wider and different readership, and 'Tristram Shandy' evokes a more intense kind of wish to believe in him, since he is not set up purely as the personification of an abstract quality. He may indeed represent 'Everyman' but we demand that his fictional character is consistent with his fictional upbringing and environment and we also demand veracity in comparison with real life. While reading a realistic novel we are constantly (albeit almost unconsciously) making little checks and comparisons to maintain our belief in the characters. Would he do that in that situation? Would she *really* react like that? Where there appears to be little or no disparity between the real and the fictional world, we accept the realistic fiction comfortably, without strain.

The time span of realistic novels, usually long, is also usually specific, i.e. years rather than weeks or hours. This is partly because psychological plausibility is called for, and this requires the progressive interaction of characters and events, by the author showing rather than telling us what happens. We see cause and effect: both the accumulation of incidents working on a character, and a character influencing events. Causal connections in a novel are more convincing than devices such as sudden revelation or coincidence which may strain our belief, but they need a longer time span to be worked out. Allied to causation is the idea of 'progress'.[15] This is perhaps particularly applicable to the nineteenth century novel, but it is also valid for many eighteenth century novels too. The protagonist progresses through many vicissitudes and misunderstandings, in the course of which he or she becomes morally educated, and this takes time. The realist novel often ends in marriage, and in retrospect the trials and adventures become a preparation for adulthood, for taking up a stable place in society. I stress that, in the classic realist novel, wisdom and maturity are gradually *achieved*; the later modernist emphasis is on the moment of illumination, the sudden enlightenment, but this is not characteristic of realism.

In the eighteenth century, Richardson came closest to achieving a sense of immediacy in his treatment of time. In his extremely long novel, *Clarissa*, the narrative takes place through the medium of letters. This epistolary technique enables him to give almost a minute-by-minute description of events, and the reader feels closely involved with what's happening. One of the technical difficulties in writing a novel is the disparity between the time span of the narrative action, and the time it takes the reader to complete the book. For example, we may take a few hours to read a novel that covers a hundred years. This is such an obvious aspect of novel-reading that we scarcely notice that a 'convention' is being employed, i.e. the artificial compression of time during the narrative process. We notice only if it's done badly, too obviously heralded by words or phrases such as 'Several years later' or 'Let us now jump thirty years.' Usually an author is much more subtle, and we accept the manipulation of time span without anxiety. Sterne, however, is fascinated by this problem and constantly draws his readers' attention to it. It becomes, in a sense, one of the main topics of *Tristram Shandy*. How do you write a convincing story if you skip several years, months, weeks or even hours? In a wonderful cry of anguish Tristram realizes the basic problem of writing his life story: 'I declare I have been at it these six weeks, making all the speed I possibly could,—and am not yet born' (I, 14, p. 65). We will examine Sterne's treatment of time in more detail in Chapter 6 of this *Guide*. By highlighting a difficulty that is usually carefully hidden, Sterne makes us aware that his fictive priorities are different from those of his contemporaries. We begin to see that literary technique is as much a part of the subject matter of *Tristram Shandy* as is the life of the hero himself.

The first problem for a novelist is 'Where do I start?' and this question obsesses the narrator in *Tristram Shandy*. Defoe and Fielding, like so many novelists who work in the realist mode, begin *Robinson Crusoe* and *Tom Jones* with the central protagonist's birth, but in *Tristram Shandy* the hero's ancestry and the influences and circumstances of his conception are given priority. As in dealing with the truncation of time, the realist author is usually concerned to hide the mechanics of selection from the reader. We may say that though selection has taken place, the narrator pretends that we are getting the whole story. Sterne, however, again makes a technical problem a central issue in *Tristram Shandy*. He cannot decide what is relevant to his plot, and he therefore makes innumerable digressions. After a while we begin to realize that the novel consists largely of digression rather than a clearly structured story line.

In the definition of realism I quoted earlier, Ian Watt talks about the 'referential use of language' as characteristic of the realist novel. In realist terms, language is assumed to be transparent. The reader seems to see the objects it refers to, and attention is drawn to them, rather than to the language itself. Unlike poetry or poetic drama, the realist novel is not highly metaphoric, and the ordinariness of its language makes it very accessible to us. It gives the illusion that there is little or no disjunction between life and art. We do not have to change gear, as it were, to read a 'realist' novel, whereas poetry makes different, and, I would argue, more intense linguistic demands on us. Sterne refuses to accept the convention of using language discreetly without drawing attention to it. *Tristram Shandy* is an extravaganza, a rich and indulgent flaunting of words for their own sake, for effect and for decoration, rather than for utilitarian purposes.

The major eighteenth-century novelists such as Defoe, Richardson and Fielding contributed in very different ways to the evolution of the 'realist' novel, a form which reached its height in the nineteenth century. Indeed, the realist text has strongly influenced our idea of what a novel is. We tend to use the nineteenth-century novel as a yardstick by which we measure other examples of the genre. We need to remember, however, that 'realism', which seems so natural, relies on conventions which are highly artificial. The majority of 'realist' novels adopt an omniscient viewpoint, and a chronological, causal narrative with a clear development. They operate on the assumption that individual characters are knowable, and that we as readers share with the author a consensus about the meaning of the words used. If you think about them, these are really very *unrealistic* premises. In real life, situations are not clarified for us by a single, clear viewpoint, and events do not fall into ordinary sequences where a specific cause leads to an equally specific effect.

People frequently behave inexplicably, or out of character, and we may have ideas about the meaning of words which are personal and not universal. In *Tristram Shandy* Sterne acknowledges and parodies the differences between reality and the conventions of realism, and our enjoyment of his novel relies to some extent on our awareness of those conventions.

Having now outlined some of the influences on Laurence Sterne, both biographical and intellectual, we can proceed to examine the ways in which he incorporates these influences in his own work. But remember, before going on further in this *Guide*, you should first complete your reading of *Tristram Shandy*.

# 3. Sentiment, Sexuality and the Reader's Role

In Chapter 1 of the *Guide* I asked you to list what had happened in the first six chapters of *Tristram Shandy*. Now that you have completed the novel, would you summarize its main plot in a few sentences.

DISCUSSION

Here, for interest, is my version of the story. How does yours compare?

Tristram Shandy, having been conceived, is born, and his nose is crushed by the doctor's forceps in the process. He is baptised and given the wrong name. His father, Walter Shandy, slowly works on an encyclopaedia for the upbringing of his son. Aged five, Tristram is accidentally circumcised by a faulty sash window. It is faulty because

Uncle Toby's servant has taken the weights to make miniature cannons for their model fortifications where Toby re-enacts the siege of Namur. The adult Tristram visits France. The Widow Wadman falls in love with Toby, and is curious to know the exact nature of the war wound to his groin. Uncle Toby is disillusioned when he learns the reason for her apparently compassionate interest.

That is a short summary for such a long novel, but do you agree that it covers the main events? In other words, *Tristram Shandy* is a novel where 'what happens' hardly at all conveys a sense of the novel's themes. I have called this chapter 'Sentiment, Sexuality and the Reader's Role' because I feel these aspects of *Tristram Shandy* show more accurately what the novel is *about* than the plot summary itself. It is a novel imbued with feeling and shot through with sexuality, and the role of the reader is made an essential part of its subject matter, since Sterne consciously invokes the reader's response in matters both sentimental and sexual.

You will have noticed that in the last sentence I substituted the word 'feeling' for that of 'sentiment'. A modern dictionary includes this definition of 'sentiment': 'a tendency or view based on or coloured with emotion' (*Concise Oxford Dictionary*). It is important to define our terms clearly, because one of the persistent criticisms of Sterne is that his work is 'sentimental'. Indeed, he called a later book *A Sentimental Journey*, and this adjective is sometimes used to denigrate *Tristram Shandy*. The term 'sentimental' is confusing, and has changed meaning since the eighteenth century. Would you now jot down quickly what the word 'sentimental' means to you?

You may have written something like: nostalgic, overemotional, maudlin, schmaltzy, sloppy or mushy, and indeed these terms indicate current usage of 'sentimental'. But in the eighteenth century the meaning was different, although it caused confusion even then. In 1749, Lady Bradshaigh asks Richardson to explain it:

> What in your opinion is the meaning of the word sentimental, so much in vogue about the polite? Everything clever and agreeable is comprehended in that word . . . I am frequently astonished to hear such a one is a *sentimental* man; we were a *sentimental* party; I have been taking a *sentimental* walk.[1]

If you look up the word 'sentimental' in a detailed dictionary, you will see the shift in meanings. In the *Shorter Oxford Dictionary* 'sentimental' in 1762 is defined as 'arising from or determined by feeling rather than reason'. It is also given as a term of literary criticism in 1762: 'Of literary compositions etc., appealing to sentiment, expressive of the tender emotions, esp. those of love'.[2] So in

order to formulate a question about the sentimentality of *Tristram Shandy*, it is perhaps better to ask two separate questions, without using the word at all. **Please would you consider the following questions:**
1. Do you find *Tristram Shandy* a novel determined by feeling rather than reason?
2. Do you find it mawkish?

## DISCUSSION

There are obviously no 'right' or 'wrong' answers. Your response will probably depend on how you react to Tristram's extreme sensibility—his capacity for intense emotion, and his readiness to empathize with others in their joy or distress. Is it genuine, or is Sterne engaged in a kind of emotional titillation? Critics have disagreed violently about this. Here are two differing reactions (In the second, although Thackeray appears to be talking about Sterne, the man, he is actually referring to his writing.):

1. There appears to have been in Sterne a vein of dry, sarcastic humour, and of extreme tenderness of feeling; the latter sometimes carried to affectation, as in the tale of Maria, and the apostrophe of the recording angel: but at other times pure, and without blemish. The story of Le Fevre [sic] is perhaps the finest in the English language. My father's restlessness, both of body and mind, is inimitable ... My uncle Toby is one of the finest compliments ever paid to human nature. (Hazlitt, 1819)[3]
2. How much was deliberate calculation and imposture—how much was false sensibility—and how much true feeling? ... I suppose Sterne had this artistic sensibility; he used to blubber perpetually in his study, and finding his tears infectious, and that they brought him a great popularity, exercised the lucrative gift of weeping; he utilized it, and cried on every occasion. I own that I don't value or respect much the cheap dribble of those fountains. He fatigues me with his perpetual disquiet and his uneasy appeals to my risible or sentimental faculties. He is always looking in my face, watching his effect, uncertain whether I think him an imposter or not; posture-making, coaxing, and imploring me. 'See what sensibility I have—own now that I'm very clever—do cry now, you can't resist this.' (Thackeray, 1854)[4]

The example most often quoted to illustrate Sterne's sensibility (for better or worse) is the story of Le Fever, Volume VI, Chapters 6–10. **Would you now reread this, and note your response to it. Do you agree with Hazlitt that it is moving, or with Thackeray that Sterne is 'watching his effect'? Or is it simply mawkish and over-emotional?**

## DISCUSSION

The story of Le Fever heralded a change in tone in *Tristram Shandy*, and on publication of Volumes V and VI it was much praised by reviewers who had become irritated at what they saw as Sterne's increasing obscenity. The tale has obvious components of emotional appeal: hunger, poverty, death, an orphaned child. Nevertheless, I find it moving rather than mawkish, because its pathos is balanced by Sterne's slightly ironic humour, and also by the ways in which the episode is used as a foil for the characterization of Uncle Toby. Le Fever is, by his very name, a deliberately unconvincing character, allegoric almost, the symbol of an illness. Like Bobby Shandy, he is invented simply to be killed off by the narrator in order to show us other people's reactions. Toby's behaviour is noble and compassionate, but its portrayal is not without humour, particularly in the dialogue between Trim and Toby where the latter refuses to believe Le Fever's nearness to death.

The final few lines are highly skilful:

> The blood and spirits of Le Fever, which were waxing cold and slow within him, and were retreating to their last citadel, the heart,—rallied back,—the film forsook his eyes for a moment,—he looked up wishfully in my uncle Toby's face,—then cast a look upon his boy,—and that *ligament*, fine as it was, was never broken.——
> Nature instantly ebbed again,—the film returned to its place,—the pulse fluttered—stopped—went on—throbbed—stopped again—moved—stopped—shall I go on?—No.'   (VI, 10, pp. 412–3)
> ('Ligament' here means a 'bond of union'.)

The military terms (retreating, rallied) are appropriate to a soldier, and the delicacy of Sterne's prose is fitted to the subtlety of Le Fever's final mute entreaty to Uncle Toby. 'Wishfully' gives us a clue to his request, and the narrator confirms that Toby looks after Le Fever's son: 'that *ligament*, fine as it was, was never broken'. And then in the final paragraph, Sterne's fluttering prose, punctuated by dashes, enacts the last feeble pulse beats of Le Fever. But again, the pathos is undercut by the narrator's reminder that this is, after all, only fiction. Le Fever's death is linked inextricably with the act of writing when the narrator says 'Shall I go on?' and the answer is 'No.' Le Fever lives as long as his pulse rate is being written about, and the cessation of the chapter is the end of his life.

I disagree with Thackeray's polarization of 'true feeling' and 'false sensibility', since what he really seems to be complaining about is Sterne's capacity to evoke emotion in his reader without necessarily experiencing it himself at the moment of writing. But this 'emotion recollected in tranquillity'[5] is a necessary technique for any artist. A combination of intense feelings with cool detachment is necessary for the process of their delineation. They do not cancel each other out, and one of Sterne's extraordinary gifts is to excite tears and laughter in quick succession without losing narrative control. All writers control their material, and I think Thackeray is irritated with Sterne because he gives away the tricks of the trade. Sterne's candour is such that he allows his awareness of literary practice to show through, which seems to me to be *less* calculating than the average writer of fiction.

Hazlitt's evaluation of the story as 'the finest in the English language' seems to me an exaggeration, but what the episode does exemplify is Sterne's tremendous faith in the human potential for goodness. Uncle Toby, above all else, is a good man. He is clearly eccentric, dangerously innocent, sexually modest to the point of stupidity, but nevertheless he is presented with uncompromising clarity as a virtuous man. To portray such simplicity of heart is unfashionable in the twentieth century, either because writers lack moral confidence, or because they imagine a readership too cynical to accept it. Nevertheless, Sterne's belief in goodness, and his persistent portrayal of it, is one of the great strengths of *Tristram Shandy*. I think it is not a sentimental novel, in the pejorative sense, but it is certainly full of sentiment, of feeling; indeed, the necessity of love, sympathy and laughter in our everyday dealings with each other is one of the central underlying themes of the novel.

\* \* \*

Another unifying theme of *Tristram Shandy* is sexuality, both explicit and implicit. Tristram's conception begins the book, and its very sparse plot includes his accidental circumcision and the Widow Wadman's passion for Uncle Toby. Toby's war wound in his groin is constantly alluded to by the narrator, but the reader, like the widow, is left to speculate about its effect on Toby's sexuality. A woman called 'dear Jenny' is sometimes mentioned in an affectionate context by Tristram, but we are never told exactly who she is. So although there are explicit sexual themes in the novel, the treatment of them is left incomplete. This is a kind of teasing by the narrator, who seems to offer several potentialities that are not brought to fruition. This theme of incompletion, which is often very funny, is introduced by the very first episode in the novel.

**Would you now turn back to Volume I, Chapter 1 of *Tristram Shandy*, and reread it. How do you account for its humour and how does it relate to the rest of the novel?**

## DISCUSSION

It is funny, surely, because of the unexpected incongruity between the action and the question. A romantic view of sexual intercourse might have had Mrs Shandy swooning with pleasure; even a realistic view might have had her distracted from mundane, practical thoughts about a clock. But clearly we are expected to infer that Mr Shandy is not a great lover, nor Mrs Shandy given to enjoyment of lovemaking. The contrast between their potential (though unrealized) bliss, and the prosaic nature of Mrs Shandy's question—and its timing—makes us laugh because it is bathetic. Romance is deflated, and Sterne, well aware of the implicit pun, leaves us with an anticlimax in several senses. This awareness of idealized sexuality (passionate, fulfilling) and its opposite (lukewarm, unsatisfying) underlies *Tristram Shandy*, and indeed, becomes a metaphor for the process of creative writing, and for the novel as a whole. On one hand, there is an ideal for writing as well as for sex; on the other, real life falls far short of those ideals, so that both sexual and literary creativity seldom really achieve what is imagined or desired. But the triumph of Sterne is that he wrests something from his failure. His material is precisely that gap, if you like, between aspiration and achievement. Always exploiting his and the reader's yearning toward perfection, using it as a foil, what he gives us is a wry and humorous acceptance of imperfect sex and imperfect sentences—a beautiful acknowledgement and acceptance of life and literature as it really is for most of us.

This first episode also relates to the rest of the novel in that Tristram's poor start in life seems to lead him into misfortune throughout the narrative. He perceives his ill luck beginning from the moment of his conception, and this determines his whole life. Tristram is an impotent character; things happen to him and around him, but he lacks the capacity to determine his own path.

Indeed, impotence is another underlying theme which unites the chaotic disparity of *Tristram Shandy*. **Can you think of the variations on this theme throughout the novel, for example in Volume IX, Chapter 11?**

## DISCUSSION

The Shandys have relegated sexual intercourse to a monthly event, but near the end of the novel there is an indication that even that is proving too much for a man of Walter's age and temperament. In Volume IX, Chapter 11 we are shown a vignette of Mr and Mrs Shandy coming out of church, and something in Mrs Shandy's tone makes Walter think about the date.

He instantly took out his almanac; but before he could untie it, Yorick's congregation coming out of church, became a full answer to one half of his business with it—and my mother telling him it was a sacrament day—left him as little in doubt, as to the other part—He put his almanac into his pocket.

The first Lord of the Treasury thinking of *ways and means*, could not have returned home, with a more embarrassed look. (IX, 11, p. 585)

In other words, Walter has realized that it is the first Sunday in the month, and is apparently not looking forward to the 'little family concernments' that this date entails.

The theme of impotence pursues poor Tristram from his conception onwards. At his birth, the narrator tells us of the damage done to his nose, with great play on the symbolism of the word 'nose'. So that, finally, after all the hints and innuendo, 'nose' comes to be indelibly associated with 'penis' in the reader's mind, and we are left with grave misgivings for both Tristram's nose and his sexual potential. He is then wrongly named, 'Tristram' being substituted for Trismegistus, a name which Walter had hoped would 'bring all things to rights' (IV, 11). And then poor Tristram, aged five, is nearly castrated (but actually only circumcised) by the falling sash window. It is no wonder, surely, that the adult narrator Tristram expresses anxiety about his sexuality, and in Volume VII, Chapter 29 he obliquely relates a sexual failure with his 'dear Jenny'. Talking of disasters, he says

> Do, my dear Jenny, tell the world for me, how I behaved under one, the most oppressive of its kind, which could befall me as a man, proud, as he ought to be, of his manhood—
> 'Tis enough, saidst thou, coming close up to me, as I stood with my garters in my hand, reflecting upon what had *not* passed—'Tis enough, Tristram, and I am satisfied, saidst thou, whispering these words in my ear, \*\*\*\* \*\* \*\*\*\* \*\*\* \*\*\*\*\*\*;—\*\*\*\* \*\* \*\*\*\*—any other man would have sunk down to the centre—
> —Everything is good for something, quoth I.
> —I'll go into Wales for six weeks, and drink goat's whey—and I'll gain seven years longer life for the accident. (VII, 29, p. 494)

The asterisks are left for the reader to fill in, as indeed Sterne frequently leaves gaps when he wishes to avoid the charge of obscenity. Again, Sterne *enacts* the theme of impotence (as well as implying it) by the incompletion of the incident which refers to it. The story, like the act, is left unfinished.

In contrast to the discreet implication of Tristram's impotence, the question of Uncle Toby's potency is central to the novel, and is not resolved for us until Volume IX, Chapter 22. We are never told

## Sentiment, Sexuality and the Reader's Role

the exact nature of his wound, but his future happiness seems to rely on Widow Wadman's estimation of his erectile functioning. Like Mr Shandy, her first husband had been 'afflicted with a sciatica' for many years, and she is clearly anxious not to have another celibate marriage. Finally, the novel ends with the suspected impotence of Walter Shandy's bull, which is kept for the cows of the whole parish. And this ending reinforces the idea of incompletion, of unachieved aspiration, which I am suggesting underlies the whole of *Tristram Shandy*. Not only is sex disappointing, but love too is illusory. *Tristram Shandy* is about solipsism, non-communication and isolation, and not even sex or love are allowed to alleviate these conditions.

This disillusion is linked with the relationships with women shown in this novel.

From your knowledge of the entire book, what would you say was Sterne's attitude to women in *Tristram Shandy*? Make notes on the narrator's descriptions of, for example, Mrs Shandy and the Widow Wadman.

DISCUSSION

Sterne's attitude to women in *Tristram Shandy* seems extremely negative. They are portrayed as stupid (Mrs Shandy), or as servants (Susannah, the scullion, Bridget), as sex-objects (Jenny, the innkeeper's daughter at Montreuil, the Beguine who ministered to Corporal Trim), or as sexually rapacious (the Widow Wadman, and Aunt Dinah, fairly openly; the Abbess of Androuillets and Margarita, unconsciously). The female reader whom the narrator calls 'Madam' is frequently used as a scapegoat, accused of professing modesty and then lambasted by the narrator because she does not have it. Poor Mrs Shandy especially bears the brunt of the hostility. She is usually shown from the point of view of her husband, Walter, and from the very first chapter is shown to be an irritant to him. In Volume I, Chapter 18, during an argument over Mrs Shandy's confinement we are asked:

> What could my father do? He was almost at his wit's end;——talked it over with her in all moods;—placed his arguments in all lights; —argued the matter with her like a christian,—like a heathen,—like a husband,—like a father,—like a patriot,—like a man:—My mother answered everything only like a woman; which was a little hard upon her;—for as she could not assume and fight it out behind such a variety of characters,—'twas no fair match;—'twas seven to one. (I, 18, p. 75)

The narrator denies Mrs Shandy the variety of roles he allows to her husband, and, thus handicapped from the beginning of the novel as 'only like a woman', she is shown henceforth as passive and bovine. Later we learn that

> it was a consuming vexation to my father, that my mother never asked the meaning of a thing she did not understand.—That she is not a woman of science [meaning 'knowledge' in this context], my father would say—is her misfortune—but she might ask a question.
> My mother never did. (VI, 39, p. 452)

Walter is aware that at times the solidarity of women is a powerful defence against men, and this is particularly evident to him when Mrs Shandy is giving birth to Tristram:

> ... from the very moment the mistress of the house is brought to bed, every female in it, from my lady's gentle-woman down to the cinder-wench, becomes an inch taller for it; and give themselves more airs upon that single inch, than all their other inches put together. (IV, 12, p. 285)

To be fair to Sterne, Toby is very sympathetic to women, and the conversation ends with a typographical illustration of the difference between Walter and Toby in their attitude to women:

> God bless ⎫ 'em all—said my uncle Toby and my father, each to
> Deuce take ⎭                          himself. (IV, 12, p. 285)

It is speculation, but appears highly likely from what we know of their marriage, that Sterne based his portrait of Mrs Shandy on his wife Elizabeth. And if you look at Sterne's drawing of his wife (reproduced on p. 31) this is perhaps more eloquent than any literary characterization within the novel itself.

The role of women in *Tristram Shandy* is mostly as a source of sexual titillation. Delicious sensations are described, pulses beat faster, and in Volume VIII, Chapter 22 Trim graphically describes the thrilling experience of being rubbed by the soft white hands of a nun, who is nursing his war wound. Women in this novel do not have philosophies or opinions of their own, but are created by the author solely for their relationships with men. In *Tristram Shandy* Sterne never gives us the conversation of a group of women on their own. His approval of women in the novel is limited to those who excite men's sexual feelings: 'dear Jenny', the Beguine, the mad girl Maria (whom he asks to compare him with a goat). If Walter Shandy represents the intellect (albeit the intellect run riot), and Toby Shandy the emotions, women seem, for the most part, to represent sexuality. This is set against the theme of male impotence, whether it is Mrs Shandy's dutiful submission to Walter's infrequent, equally

3  Caricature of Sterne's wife, reputedly by Sterne

duteous matrimonial rights (in which he takes no pleasure), or the Widow Wadman's active pursuance of a sexual relationship with Uncle Toby. Walter Shandy says to his wife in front of Yorick

> 'That the devil was in women, and the whole of the affair was lust;' ... every evil and disorder in the world, of what kind and nature soever, from the first fall of Adam, down to my uncle Toby's (inclusive) was owing one way or other to the same unruly appetite. (IX, 32, p. 613)

In the next chapter he expresses his exasperation that the continuance of the human race should be dependent on such a base passion,

> ... a passion, my dear, continued my father, addressing himself to my mother, which couples and equals wise men with fools, and makes us come out of our caverns and hiding-places more like satyrs and four-footed beasts than men. (IX, 33, pp. 613–4)

I am not suggesting that Walter Shandy's contempt for women and sex wholly represents Sterne's views on the same subjects. These are perhaps more accurately represented by the narrator in Volume VIII, Chapters 11–13, where he describes the pains and pleasures of being in love. Love is described as the most 'lyrical of all human passions', but even so, the pains far outweigh the pleasures. Women are 'trouble' for the narrator of *Tristram Shandy*, just as in real life the liaisons of the married clergyman, Laurence Sterne, were a great source of trouble for him.

Since both Walter and Toby (from distaste and modesty respectively) are less than positive about sex, what then happens to their own sexuality? **Please read the following quotations: the first is about Toby's bowling-green, adapted for his war games. The second is about Walter's purchase of a rare book by a French writer, Bruscambille. When you have read them, note what is significant about their language.**

> 1 ... as Trim uttered the words, 'A rood and a half of ground to do what they would with:'—this identical bowling green instantly presented itself, and became curiously painted, all at once, upon the retina of my uncle Toby's fancy;—which was the physical cause of making him change colour, or at least, of heightening his blush to that immoderate degree I spoke of.
> 
> Never did lover post down to a beloved mistress with more heat and expectation, than my uncle Toby did, to enjoy this self-same thing in private ... (II, 5, p. 118)
>
> 2 ... he gave no more for Bruscambille than three half-crowns, owing indeed to the strong fancy which the stall-man saw my father had for the book the moment he laid his hands upon it.—There are not three Bruscambilles in Christendom,—said the stall-man, except what are chained up in the libraries of the curious. My father flung down the money as quick as lightning,—took Bruscambille into his bosom,—hied home from Piccadilly to Coleman Street with it, as he would have hied home with a treasure, without taking his hand once off from Bruscambille all the way.
>
> ... when my father got home, he solaced himself with Bruscambille after the manner, in which, 'tis ten to one, your worship solaced yourself with your first mistress,——that is, from morning even unto night: (III, 35, p. 231)

## DISCUSSION

Sterne himself gives us the sexual analogy explicit in each case, and the language of each extract reinforces it.[6] In the first quotation, the words 'do what they would with' cause Toby to blush, and the phrase 'curiously painted' sounds almost like his impression of the face of a prostitute. Although Toby is very modest, the narrator is very well aware of unconscious associations in his mind. The words 'lover', 'beloved mistress', 'heat', 'expectation', 'enjoy', 'thing', 'in private' spell out clearly the intensity of Toby's involvement with his fortifications. In his passion for war games, Toby's sexuality has been displaced from women to his hobby-horse—a phrase which itself had the colloquial meaning of 'whore'.

The description of Walter's book purchase is also sexually suggestive. Phrases such as 'strong fancy', 'laid his hands upon it', 'took ... into his bosom', 'without taking his hands once off ...', 'solaced himself with' all underline the implicit identification of 'book' with 'mistress'. The whole episode is analogous to buying the services of a prostitute, but Walter is clearly much more excited about a book than about any woman, and his sexual drive is displaced from women to words.

Similarly, I would suggest, the narrator Tristram channels his sexual energies into the writing of his *Life and Opinions*. He draws frequent parallels between sex, procreation and the creation of a book. Tristram's (mis)conception is also the start of the novel, and his sexual impotence parallels his difficulties in writing a realist novel. Writing is sometimes described as masturbatory: 'Matter grows under our hands' (V, 16, p. 366), and terminology about a novel's structure has sexual connotations. In talking of narrative, Tristram says a writer 'may go backwards and forwards as he will' (V, 25, p. 375) and this metaphor is later elaborated: 'when a man is telling a story in the strange way I do mine, he is obliged continually to be going backwards and forwards to keep all tight together in the reader's fancy' (VI, 33, p. 444). He then refers to the 'darkest passages' and quotes a Latin sentence meaning 'how much more careful we should be when begetting children', referring of course to his own conception and to the creation of a novel.

This analogy between the movements of sex and the movement of Tristram's narrative is used by him as a justification for not pursuing a straightforward, linear progression. Digressions give pleasure, it is implied, both to writer and reader, and enjoying the telling of the story is as important as arriving at its ending. Typically (as I mentioned earlier in this chapter) *Tristram Shandy* ends in an anticlimax, a kind of literary *coitus interruptus*, which parallels the interrupted sexual act at the beginning of the novel.

\* \* \*

Throughout *Tristram Shandy* Sterne relies heavily on the role of the reader, which becomes one of the unifying themes of the novel in two ways: first, by the recurrent device of addressing the reader, who then becomes an important character in the text, and secondly, by the sense-making and unifying procedure that the reader is persuaded to engage in: filling in the gaps, imagining what is merely implied through Sterne's use of the *double entendre*, making chronological and causal connections, which Sterne has omitted or transposed. In recent literary criticism there has been a great deal of interest in the reader's response to a text.[7] All novels necessarily depend on the reader's response for their meaning, and all novelists have in mind an image of the ideal reader, whether or not such a person is addressed rhetorically within the novel. But here I intend to help you to focus specifically on the ways in which Sterne openly manipulates the concept of the reader's role within *Tristram Shandy*. From the beginning of the novel he insists on the reader's importance in completing the meaning of the novel:

> The truest respect which you can pay to the reader's understanding, is to halve this matter amicably, and leave him something to imagine, in his turn, as well as yourself.
>
> For my own part, I am eternally paying him compliments of this kind, and do all that lies in my power to keep his imagination as busy as my own. (II, 11, p. 127)

To this end we are frequently asked to participate in the literary process. Sterne often exhorts his readers to use their imaginations: 'Imagine to yourself a little, squat, uncourtly figure . . .' (II, 9, p. 123); 'My father, as any body may naturally imagine . . .' (I, 16, p. 69). But he goes further than this: he leaves out words, indicating them by asterisks or dashes, so that the reader is forced into active participation not only in the reading, but, as it were, in the writing of the novel. Sterne does this in a variety of ways, and the response demanded of the reader varies according to his techniques of omission.

**Would you look at the following examples where words are deliberately omitted by Sterne. How do you 'read' them? What are the differences between them, not just typographically, but in the implied role of the reader for each one?**

1 The chamber-maid had left no \*\*\*\*\*\*\* \*\*\* under the bed:
—Cannot you contrive, master, quoth Susannah, lifting up the sash with one hand, as she spoke, and helping me up into the window-seat with the other,—cannot you manage, my dear, for a single time, to \*\*\*\* \*\*\* \*\* \*\*\* \*\*\*\*\*\*? (V, 17, p. 369)
2 . . . With a kick of both heels at once, but at the same time the most natural kick that could be kicked in her situation—for supposing \*\*\*\*\*\* \*\*\* to be the sun in its meridian, it was a north-east kick—she kicked the pin out of her fingers—the *etiquette* which hung upon it, down—down it fell to the ground, and was shivered into a thousand atoms. (VIII, 9, p. 524)

3   —Lord have mercy upon me,—said my father to himself—
    * * * * * * * * * *
    * * * * * * * * * *
    * * * * * * * * * *
    * * * * * * * * * *
    * * * * * * *

(VI, 39, p. 453)

## DISCUSSION

In the first extract the asterisks relate to specific letters or words, and it is comparatively easy to work out the implied text. I imagine that we are meant to substitute the words 'chamber-pot' and 'piss out of the window' to make the sentence complete. By getting the reader to supply this slightly indelicate suggestion Sterne deftly avoids the charge of bawdiness himself. In the second extract, however, it is much more difficult to fill in the meaning of the asterisks, and although we may feel that Sterne is alluding to specific words, the context does not enable us to guess them easily. This example is similar to the allusion of impotence I mentioned earlier in this chapter, where it is also difficult to transliterate the asterisks exactly. So here the reader is left freer than in the first extract to 'read into' the text, rather than merely to read it. We shall never know what Sterne actually had in mind, and we have to substitute an approximation. In this way Sterne is acknowledging and almost parodying the problem of ordinary communication by words, which I talked about in Chapter 2 of this *Guide*: that is, how can we ever be sure that the same word conveys the same meaning to one another? Here, Sterne is making a joke about the imprecision of intended and received meanings. If words are not a totally reliable means of communication anyway, why not substitute asterisks and allow the reader to make an approximation of the meaning? Thus 'reading' a novel in these terms sometimes means 'writing' it as well. In engaging with *Tristram Shandy* the reader has a creative as well as a receptive role, and this links with the definition of writing that Sterne gives us quite early on in the novel: 'Writing, when properly managed, (as you may be sure I think mine is), is but a different name for conversation:' (II, 11, p. 127).

The third extract consists of five rows of asterisks, but there is no direct correlation between them and the specific words they might represent. The reader can only infer what Walter's thoughts might be, and there is no contextual pressure from the narrator to come to a definite conclusion about the meaning implied. Certainly we have already been given sufficient information about Walter Shandy's attitude to the procreation, birth and upbringing of children to make an intelligent guess at his views on the subject. But there is freedom left for the reader to interpret the asterisks with some latitude.

Here is a further, more complex group of examples. See what you make of each of them before proceeding to my comments.

4 ... my uncle Toby hummed over the letter. ——— ——— ——— ——— ——— ——— ——— ——— ——— ——— ——— ——— ——— ——— ——— ——— ——— ——— —he's gone! said my uncle Toby.—Where—Who? cried my father.—My nephew, said my uncle Toby.—What—without leave—without money—without governor? cried my father in amazement. No:—he is dead, my dear brother, quoth my uncle Toby.— (V, 2, p. 346)

5 ... it then presently occurred to me, that I had left my remarks in the pocket of the chaise—and that in selling my chaise, I had sold my remarks along with it, to the chaise-vamper. I leave this void space that the reader may swear into it any oath that he is most accustomed to— (VIII, 37, p. 504)

6 To conceive this right,—call for pen and ink—here's paper ready to your hand.—Sit down, Sir, paint her to your own mind—as like your mistress as you can—as unlike your wife as your conscience will let you—'tis all one to me—please put your own fancy in it.

# Sentiment, Sexuality and the Reader's Role

————Was ever any thing in Nature so sweet!——so exquisite!——
Then, dear Sir, how could my uncle Toby resist it?

Thrice happy book! thou wilt have one page, at least, within thy covers, which MALICE will not blacken and which IGNORANCE cannot misrepresent.   (VI, 38, p. 452)

In the fourth extract, dashes replace the asterisks, and they represent the content of the letter that Walter has casually asked Toby to read to him. We can deduce the material in the letter—the news of Bobby Shandy's death—from the subsequent conversation between Toby and Walter, although we are given no clues at all about the wording of it. But do you notice how meticulously the dashes imitate the actual rhythm of Toby's *reading*? It is almost possible to imagine the emotions engendered by the nonexistent text. The dashes of the first two lines are spaced almost evenly, and then the spaces in the third line are longer, indicating a slowing down, a disbelief, as if it were difficult for Toby to take in the meaning. Then in the last line the dashes are closer together as if the import of the letter suddenly rushes into Toby's mind. It is an intensely subtle way of conveying the experience of reading an alarming letter, and very easy for the reader of *Tristram Shandy* to miss if you simply skip over the sections where words are missed out, as being unimportant. Sterne is saying, in effect, that words are not the only means of eloquence, and we will see in the next chapter of this *Guide* how much gestures and attitudes are used to convey meaning also. Here, the meaning of individual words is sacrificed to a typographical enactment of Toby's act of reading and absorbing shocking information. But, and I want to stress the point, meaning *is* still conveyed to the reader, in the form of a vivid and realistic impression.

Sterne's technique in the fifth extract is to leave two-thirds of a line blank for the reader to write in or, more surrealistically, 'to swear into it', his or her oath. This is a very literal way of sharing the task of writing with the reader and, indeed, of suggesting that the reader can fill in the gaps orally if preferred. Thus the book becomes more than simply writing or potential writing; the medium of communication is extended to include speech. In the final example this blank line is taken much further, as it were, in Volume VI, Chapter 38. Sterne leaves a blank page for the reader to draw in his or her own version of the Widow Wadman. The narrator uses the term 'paint', and the materials offered are 'pen and ink', so that we may assume that the portrait could be in words or as a drawing. Then, after the blank page, the narrator assumes an exquisite picture has been drawn, and reacts to it appropriately. The medium of words has here been extended to that of fine art, again showing how extraordinarily flexible Sterne is, and how he refuses to grant words any exclusivity as means of communication within a novel.

Sterne's use of asterisks, dashes or blank pages forces the reader to participate in the creative process, and a perpetual game with the reader's response is an integral part of *Tristram Shandy*. A further part of this game is Sterne's heavy reliance on the use of the *double entendre* to create a subtext, usually of sexual meaning, without having to commit himself to it openly. The first episode of *Tristram Shandy*, in which sexual intercourse is interrupted by a query about the winding of a clock, itself became a *double entendre*. A facetious article entitled *The Clockmaker's Outcry Against the Author of 'The Life and Opinions of Tristram Shandy'* was published on 9 May, 1760. In it the author (purporting to be a clockmaker) complains that Sterne has brought his profession into disrepute. 'The directions I had for making several clocks for the country are countermanded; because no modest lady now dares to mention a word about winding-up a clock, without exposing herself to the sly leers and jokes of the family, to her frequent confusion. Nay, the common expression of street-walkers is 'Sir, will you have your clock wound-up?' Alas, reputable, venerable clocks, that have flourished for ages, are ordered to be taken down by virtuous matrons, and be disposed of as obscene lumber, exciting to acts of carnality!'[8] Sterne and clocks were the talk of fashionable London in the summer of 1760, and he delighted in his fame.

**In order to see how blatantly Sterne uses the *double entrendre*, would you now reread Volume II, Chapters 6 and 7. What is the reader's role in those two chapters?**

DISCUSSION

In order for these chapters to be understood, the reader needs to have what Ian Watt has called 'a normally contaminated mind'.[9] A totally innocent reader will miss half the implied meanings of *Tristram Shandy* since they so often rely on an understanding of obscenity. So the reader's role in Chapter 6 is to supply the colloquialism for vagina, 'cunt', which Sterne avoids by asterisks which in Volume VI, Chapter 33 he calls 'stars . . . I hang up in some of the darkest passages'. The extended joke of this chapter is to force the reader to provide the word which Sterne 'innocently' avoids. By relying on his reader's understanding of the implied obscenity the narrator can still protest his own innocence, and yet communicate the bawdy implications of his narrative. In Volume II, Chapter 7 the reader is expected to understand explicitly the unconscious connection made by Uncle Toby between the small crevice in the chimneypiece, and the 'Right end of a woman'. Unless we, as readers, understand Sterne is implying 'vagina' by 'crevice', then the anecdote loses its meaning. We need to appreciate the humorous contrast between the genuine modesty of Uncle Toby's conscious mind, and the accurate sexual deductions of his unconscious. So the reader's role is to supply the linking explanation that Sterne omits, and thus, in a sense, to help Sterne to 'write' the novel.

Sterne wickedly exploits the *double entendre* to its limit in Volume III, Chapter 31, where he introduces the subject of noses. By insisting that he is not using the word to invoke another meaning, he effectively induces his reader to give it a phallic significance:

> I define a nose as follows—entreating only beforehand, and beseeching my readers, both male and female, of what age, complexion, and condition soever, for the love of God and their own souls, to guard against the temptations and suggestions of the devil, and suffer him by no art or wile to put any other ideas into their minds, than what I put into my definition.—For by the word *Nose*, throughout all this

long chapter of noses, and in every other part of my work, where the word *Nose* occurs,—I declare, by that word I mean a Nose, and nothing more, or less. (III, 31, p. 225)

Having led the reader on, Sterne is quite capable of turning round and attacking him or her. For example, after pages about noses where the word 'penis' lurks in the punning sub-text, Sterne addresses the reader directly:

——Fair and softly, gentle reader!——where is thy fancy carrying thee?—If there is truth in man, by my great-grandfather's nose, I mean the external organ of smelling, or that part of man which stands prominent in his face,—and which painters say, in good jolly noses and well-proportioned faces, should comprehend a full third,—that is, measuring downwards from the setting on of the hair.—
—What a life of it has an author, at this pass! (III, 33, p. 228)

The outrageous aspect of this mock accusation and innocence is that Sterne still contrives to continue his pubic pun ('measuring downwards from the setting on of the hair') even while complaining of the reader's over-active imagination.

One of the best examples of the *double entendre* leading to a crucial misunderstanding is the Widow Wadman's concern about the nature of Uncle Toby's war wound in his groin.

—And whereabouts, dear Sir, quoth Mrs Wadman, a little categorically, did you receive this sad blow?—In asking this question, Mrs Wadman gave a slight glance towards the waistband of my Uncle Toby's red plush breeches, expecting naturally, as the shortest reply to it, that my Uncle Toby would lay his forefinger upon the place— (IX, 26, p. 607)

Uncle Toby understands her to be enquiring whereabouts in Namur he was injured, and consequently sends Trim up to the attic to fetch a map of the town to show the widow the exact spot. The humour of this lies in our appreciation of the widow's sexual expectations, and Toby's innocent ignorance of them. The difference between the anatomical and geographical implications of the word 'place' is comically exploited by Sterne, and in this case the reader is invited to share the joke at Uncle Toby's expense, rather than, as so often, being the victim of it.

Some critics have complained of Sterne's hypocrisy, and of his slyness in utilizing the 'contaminated' minds of his readers. How do you feel about this? I feel that Sterne exploits us lightheartedly and with good humour, so that in fact one of the purposes of *Tristram Shandy* is to teach us to laugh at ourselves. Indeed, it is possible to grant Sterne's bawdiness and *double entendres* a serious didactic purpose, i.e. of forcing his readers to confront their own hypocrisy, to abandon any holier-than-thou stance we might have, and to admit our common humanity. This seems to me to be more nearly in accordance with Sterne's viewpoint than a simple, narrow-minded desire to shock people through obscenity.

\* \* \*

In this chapter I have looked at themes which recur throughout *Tristram Shandy*. As we have seen, there is very little plot in this novel. It is rather a work which appeals to the feelings, and encourages the reader's participation in a variety of original and unusual ways. It has an atmosphere of sexuality, but just as there is very little effective plot in *Tristram Shandy*, so there is very little effective sex. Instead, the text glimmers with sexual expectations—hints, glances, innuendoes, half-finished sentences—which are rapidly succeeded by disillusion. The impossibility of communication—of sexual and literary satisfaction—is its theme, combined with an eloquent and unremitting yearning for them both.

# 4. Characterization

What do you understand by the concept of 'character' in a novel? Take a blank piece of paper, and 'brain-storm' for one minute, i.e. jot down quickly anything that comes into your mind.

DISCUSSION

This is my unedited list: people, relating, foibles, appearances, doing things, idiosyncratic, individuals, differences, quirks, credible, like us/not like us, consistent/inconsistent, do appearances = true person? difficulty of knowing, novelist knows, selection.

Yours will be different, but I would guess that what it adds up to is something about people with different personalities interacting. Characterization—the fictional presentation of people—seems intrinsic to the realist novel. Of all the novel's components such as structure, plot, narrative, setting, action, it is, I suggest, characterization that is the most immediate. If you think of novels you've read, it's more likely that you'll remember what made the characters interesting, rather than the setting or the plot. This emphasis varies: in a detective novel the intricacies of the plot may predominate; in a thriller the action is often the most important aspect. But in most novels the plot and the action are clearly shown to interweave with aspects of character, each influencing and affecting the other.

Although a person in a novel may seem more real to us than the plot in which she or he takes part, it's important to remember that, like the rest of the novel, a character is a construct of words over which the author has laboured. In this section I want you to look at Sterne's methods of characterization in *Tristram Shandy*. To enable you to do this, I shall offer comparisons with other novelists, and select passages from *Tristram Shandy* to see what effects Sterne achieves, and how.

**The following extracts are all first descriptions of characters from novels. Would you now read them carefully, and make notes about each one, based on the following questions:**

1 What is your impression of the character described?
2 Which words or phrases contribute to the impression?
3 What is the character of the narrator? Can you trust him or her? What is the relationship with the reader? Which words or phrases are especially relevant to establishing that relationship?

(a) In that part of the western division of this kingdom, which is commonly called Somersetshire, there lately lived (and perhaps lives still) a gentleman whose name was Allworthy, and who might well be called the favourite of both Nature and Fortune; for both of these seem to have contended which should bless and enrich him most. In this contention, Nature may seem to some to have come off victorious, as she bestowed on him many gifts; while Fortune had only one gift in her power; but in pouring forth this, she was so very profuse, that others perhaps may think this single endowment to have been more than equivalent to all the various blessings which he enjoyed from Nature. From the former of these, he derived an agreeable person, a sound constitution, a solid understanding, and a benevolent heart; by the latter, he was decreed to the inheritance of one of the largest estates in the county.[1]

(b) Mary Garth . . . was brown; her curly dark hair was rough and stubborn; her stature was low; and it would not be true to declare, in satisfactory antithesis, that she had all the virtues. Plainness has its peculiar temptations and vices quite as much as beauty; it is apt either to feign amiability, or, not feigning it, to show all the repulsiveness of discontent: at any rate, to be called an ugly thing in contrast with that lovely creature your companion, is apt to produce some effect beyond a sense of fine veracity and fitness in the phrase. At the age of two-and-twenty Mary had certainly not attained that perfect good sense and good principle which are usually recommended to the less fortunate girl, as if they were to be obtained in quantities ready mixed, with a flavour of resignation as required. Her shrewdness had a streak of satiric bitterness continually renewed and never carried utterly out of sight, except by a strong current of gratitude towards those who, instead of telling her that she ought to be contented, did something to make her so. Advancing womanhood had tempered her plainness, which was of a good human sort, such as the mothers of our race have very commonly worn in all latitudes under a more or less becoming headgear. Rembrandt would have painted her with pleasure, and would have made her broad features look out of the canvas with intelligent honesty. For honesty, truth-telling fairness, was Mary's reigning virtue: she neither tried to create illusions, nor indulged in them for her own behoof, and when she was in a good mood she had humour enough in her to laugh at herself.[2]

(c) My uncle, TOBY SHANDY, Madam, was a gentleman, who, with the virtues which usually constitute the character of a man of honour and rectitude,—possessed one in a very eminent degree, which is seldom or never put into the catalogue; and that was a most extreme and unparalleled modesty of nature;—though I correct the word nature, for this reason, that I may not prejudice a point which must shortly come to a hearing, and that is, Whether this modesty of his was natural or acquired.—Whichever way my uncle Toby came by it, 'twas nevertheless modesty in the truest sense of it; and that is, Madam, not in regard to words, for he was so unhappy as to have very little choice in them,—but to things;—and this kind of modesty so possessed him, and it arose to such a height in him, as almost to equal, if such a thing could be, even the modesty of a woman: That female nicety, Madam, and inward cleanliness of mind and fancy, in your sex, which makes you so much the awe of ours.[3]

## DISCUSSION

(a) My impression of Mr Allworthy is that he seems almost too good to be true! In fact my view of him isn't really very precise. From his allegorical name, All-worthy, I take him to represent worthiness, and from the last sentence I deduce that he is pleasant, healthy, wise and kind. But I have no idea of what he looks like, nor enough specific detail to give me a clear picture of him. So he's almost a symbolic figure, rather than a character I believe in.

Can I trust the narrator? I think so: the tone is very confident, and the passage is not ironic or satirical, although the personification of 'Nature' and 'Fortune' is perhaps rather flowery for a twentieth-century reader. The narrator makes certain assumptions about his or her readers, i.e. that they are compatriots ('this kingdom'); that they understand what a 'gentleman' is, and that they will accept the composition of character as a combination of 'Nature' and 'Fortune'. Nevertheless, the narrator is not totally dogmatic, or is it just that he is taking great pains not to appear to be? Some phrases seem to invite the reader's opinion, or indicate that a hypothesis is offered rather than hard facts given. For example, 'is commonly called', 'perhaps', 'might well be called', 'seem to have contended', 'may seem to some', 'others perhaps may think'. But the tone changes in the last sentence and becomes very specific, almost as if (I'm beginning to think) the narrator *has* been teasing us a little, been persuasive and lyrical up to now, so that we may be surprised by the brisk, prosaic tone of the final description. The adjective-noun list of Allworthy's qualities, and the strong, balanced sentence 'From the former ... by the latter ...' give it judicial weight, rhythm and authority.

(b) My impression of Mary Garth is that she is twenty-two years old, short and dark, and not particularly good-looking. She is strong-minded, intelligent, and somewhat bitter at her lot. She is realistic and honest, and has a sense of humour. She is able to respond warmly to people. The words which lead me to deduce these characteristics are 'brown', 'curly dark hair', 'rough and stubborn' —this, although applied to her hair, is difficult to confine to it, since stubborn is a human characteristic. It is this word 'stubborn' which led me to think that Mary is strong-minded. Other words which contribute to my impression include 'plainness', 'shrewdness', 'bitterness', 'strong currents of gratitude', 'intelligent honesty', 'never tried to create illusions, nor indulged in them', and 'humour'.

The narrator seems authoritative, self-confident. The narration varies between giving us Mary's external appearance and inward character, and generalizations about beauty and plainness. I feel that I do trust the narrator of this passage, except that there is a sharpness about the narration which echoes that of Mary's character. The narrator draws attention to her or his own veracity by explicitly refusing to compromise on truth for the sake of form ('it would not be true to declare, in satisfactory antithesis, that she had all the virtues'). Nevertheless, s/he is on Mary's side overall; any defects in her character are excused sympathetically, or balanced with good qualities. There is little overt attempt to build up a relationship with the reader, but it is assumed that certain views are shared, and these

## Characterization

are indicated by phrases such as 'that perfect good sense', and 'usually recommended'. It is also assumed that not only do we know who Rembrandt is, but also his preferred subject matter and style of painting.

(c) My impression of Toby Shandy from this extract is very hazy, except that he is a good man, extremely modest, and that this quality for some reason takes precedence over the others. There is no mention of his appearance, and the name seems rather comic. The words 'gentleman' and 'honour and rectitude' contribute to my impression of Uncle Toby's character, but the word 'modesty' occurs five times, and by the end of the description that is what seems important. The first-person narration is meandering, and there are two digressions even in this short passage. But it is also pedantic, as if the narrator were trying to pin down an elusive thought accurately. The passage consists of only two sentences, and the syntax echoes its somewhat breathless quality; semicolons and dashes divide the subordinate clauses, as if a full stop would inappropriately interrupt the flow of thought. The narrator is apparently spontaneous—'though I correct the word nature'—and it's as if this were part of a conversation, or a stream of unedited thought. There is an awareness by the narrator that this description is somewhat out of the ordinary, since he's describing a quality 'which is seldom or never put into the catalogue'. It is made clear in the last line that the narrator is a man, and the tone of this passage, for all its wandering, is confident and authoritative. A relationship is established with an imaginary woman reader by calling her Madam, and it enables the narrator to address her directly: 'your sex', 'you'.

Can we trust this narrator? He seems almost fanatically concerned to be scrupulously truthful, for example, in the phrase 'that I may not prejudge a point which must shortly come to a hearing . . .'. I certainly believe his account of Uncle Toby's modesty, although I'm bemused by his emphasis on it. But the last two lines make me uneasy. There is an ironic tone to them, heralded, I think, by the phrase 'if such a thing could be'. The modesty of women is exaggerated, parodied a little, so that the final gallantry seems like a veiled insult. And, am I imagining it, but is there not a suggestion of a sexual *double entendre* in the last four lines? If so, this undercuts the whole extract, since its subject is modesty and the narrator's admiration of it. And, further, if I as a woman reader detect a subtle sexual joke, this acts as an ironic contradiction to Sterne's insistence on the modesty of women. As I indicated in Chapter 1, as readers we are not only involved with this text; we are *entangled* in it.

\* \* \*

I have noted that all three novelists are confident in portraying character. Their emphases, however, are different. Fielding's rather brisk and external approach to his characters is exemplified in this extract. He is not concerned to build up a painstaking, realistic picture of Allworthy. He doesn't mention his appearance, or invite us to verify his character by comparisons. The name 'Allworthy' is really the sum total of all we need to know about the man, because in *Tom Jones* the development of individual character is subordinated to the demands of the complex plot.

George Eliot is very different. Unlike Fielding or Sterne there is an earnestness in her tone. It seems important to her that we believe in Mary Garth, and she works hard in making her convincing. She refuses the easy temptation of making her good because she is plain, and Mary comes over as a more complex character than Mr Allworthy or Uncle Toby.[4] She emphasizes development of character, and in this description of Mary Garth neither looks nor personality are considered to be static, set for all time. Her people are never mere pawns to be shifted around according to the mechanics of plot. *Middlemarch* is a novel about moral education, about growth and change, and consequently the investment in character and its potential is very high.

As contemporaries, Fielding and Sterne cannot help but share certain cultural assumptions; for example, their use of the word 'nature' in these extracts is very similar. But Sterne does not present stock characters or have them act as symbols in an elaborate plot. He alludes swiftly and vaguely to Uncle Toby's virtues, which 'constitute the character of a man of honour' (assuming that the reader will know what these are), and then concentrates almost obsessively on one character trait, his modesty. And, unlike George Eliot, there is no attempt at setting forth all aspects of a character in order to arrive at the 'truth'. In Volume I, Chapter 23, two chapters after this description of Uncle Toby, we are given the narrator's difficulties in the portrayal of character. Tristram wishes that a 'Momus glass'—a window—could be set in the human breast, so that the soul could be observed:

> That had the said glass been there set up, nothing more would have been wanting, in order to have taken a man's character, but to have taken a chair and gone softly, as you would to a dioptrical bee-hive, and looked in,—viewed the soul stark naked;—observed all her motions,—her machinations;—traced all her maggots from their first engendering to their crawling forth;—watch her loose in her frisks, her gambols, her capricios; and after some notice of her more solemn deportment, consequent upon such frisks, &c——then taken your pen and ink and set down nothing but what you have seen, and could

# Characterization

have sworn to:—But this is an advantage not to be had by the biographer in this planet. (I, 23, p. 96)

**Would you now reread that quotation, and ask yourself how it links up with the narrator's viewpoint in *Tristram Shandy*. What is the implication of the word 'biographer'?**

## DISCUSSION

Throughout *Tristram Shandy* Sterne uses a first-person narrator, so that everything and everyone is seen refracted, as it were, through the perception of Tristram himself. Sometimes this limitation is transcended, but usually Sterne does not have the advantage of a truly 'omniscient' narrator who claims to see 'the soul stark naked' and who can give us a character's interior thoughts and feelings. Although Tristram does tell us details about Uncle Toby's and his father's characters, they are traits deduced from a lifetime of watching their behaviour. By limiting his narratorial perspective, Sterne is making a statement about real-life difficulties in assessing character, a theme he reiterates in the novel. By using the word 'biographer' rather than 'writer' or 'novelist' Sterne maintains the illusion that Tristram, the narrator, is observing real people, and writing, not fiction, but his autobiography.

So if a writer cannot see into people, how can character be delineated?

> ... our minds shine not through the body, but are wrapt up here in a dark covering of uncrystallized flesh and blood: so that, if we would come to the specific characters of them, we must go some other way to work. (I, 23, p. 97)

Sterne therefore focuses much of his characterization on the portrayal of a dominant trait, which to him is as accurate an indication of personality as a carefully-rounded, balanced description. We get to know people in more ways than 'realist' conventions can cope with: in fits and starts, through an obsession, by things that are never said, by incessant repetitions. It is only in realist fiction that a character is built up gradually, with logical and causal progression. This concept of character requires that he or she is knowable to the reader, according to information given to us by the narrator. A novelist, for the sake of economy, cannot have a character behave totally *out* of character; it would either require too much explanation or leave the reader indignant that this uncharacteristic action was left unaccounted for.

Sterne both acknowledges and bypasses this problem by not

attempting to present character as coherent and ultimately comprehensible. In a letter written shortly after the publication of the first volumes of *Tristram Shandy* he said, 'The ruleing passion *et les égarements du coeur*, [and the strayings of the heart] are the very things which mark, and distinguish a man's character'.[5] The narrator, then, decides that he will 'draw my uncle Toby's character from his HOBBY-HORSE', suggesting implicitly that this kind of irrationality is a better guide to Uncle Toby than any attempt to understand him from a more rational standpoint. His obsession with war games, combined with his extreme modesty and gentle nature, is a paradox which Sterne continually presents, but declines to explain. Toby has the opacity of a real-life character, and is also simultaneously convincing, so that Sterne's refusal to confirm with the conventions of 'realist' characterization actually makes Toby more, not less, life-like.

As a method of characterization Sterne also concentrates on the description of external signs, gestures and attitudes of his fictional people. This information is supplemented by having Tristram the narrator convey to us his privileged knowledge of his father and his uncle.

Would you now reread Volume II, Chapter 12. First, make a list of 'direct' information about Walter Shandy *told* to us by the narrator, and then 'indirect' information which is *shown* to us by Walter's behaviour. Then do the same for Toby Shandy.

DISCUSSION

'*Direct' information:* We are told that Walter Shandy hates puns, and 'would grow testy' at the mention of one (p. 129). Later we are told directly of Walter's character: 'acute and quick sensibility', 'a little soreness of temper' which is more peevish than malignant. He is 'frank and generous' in his nature and feels pain at his outbursts, particularly those towards his brother (p. 132).
'*Indirect' information:* In this chapter we are shown Walter's impatience with his brother's obsession with fortifications. He questions Toby 'testily' (p. 129), sighs during his explanations, and then bursts out with impatience (p. 130). We see Walter 'seizing hold of both my uncle Toby's hands', begging his pardon for his 'rash humour' (p. 132). In his subsequent speech to Toby we learn of Walter's affection for him (p. 133).
'*Direct' information:* We are told of Toby's patience and courage, and of his sensitive but placid nature (pp. 130–1).
'*Indirect' information:* The anecdote of the fly, the description of

Toby's countenance as 'placid' and 'fraternal' (p. 132), and the reconciliation with Walter (p. 133).

So this chapter veers between the narrator giving us facts about the characters and showing us incidents to substantiate the facts. In this passage Sterne's methods accord with Locke's conception of empiricism in that most of the information given to us about Uncle Toby is deductive, i.e. it is deduced by the narrator from the evidence of his behaviour. In the first paragraph we're reminded that we've already been told that he's a 'man of courage'; and the narrator goes on to express his own confidence in Toby. We are seeing Toby Shandy through the perception of Tristram. He goes on to tell us what appears to be omniscient information, that he was 'of a peaceful, placid nature', and wouldn't hurt a fly. But suddenly the cliché is enlivened, given flesh as it were, by a literal example to illustrate Toby's gentleness. In one of the most famous paragraphs of *Tristram Shandy* Toby lets a fly out of the window: '—go, poor devil, get thee gone, why should I hurt thee?—This world surely is wide enough to hold both thee and me.' (II, 12, p. 131) Then follows a paragraph about the narrator's sensations on witnessing this action, which has the effect of reinforcing the quality of the action. In other words, the incident is given moral weight, not by an impersonal narrator telling us what a fine character Toby is, but by Tristram describing the beneficial effect of the action on him.

Tristram tells us of the character of his father, and again, gives us some 'inside' information in case we have any doubts about Walter's affection for his brother Toby—'whom he truly loved' (p. 132). But again, instead of asking the reader to take this on trust, the narrator gives a concrete example of their affection. He describes, not Toby's character, but his countenance: 'spread over with so much good nature:—so placid;—so fraternal—so inexpressibly tender towards him;' and its effect: 'It penetrated my father to his heart' (p. 132). Whereupon Walter begs Toby's pardon for mocking his war game, and is immediately forgiven.

Do you see how little is offered in that chapter in the way of characterization that is not substantiated by a literal example, or validated by its effect on Tristram himself? Time and again Sterne gives us an external delineation of character, either by describing appearance, features, or gestures, or by relaying the effect of one person upon another. Sometimes a foible or idiosyncracy acts as a leitmotif throughout the novel, as with Uncle Toby's whistling of 'Lillabullaro'. In Volume I we are told: 'You must know it was the usual channel through which his passions got vent, when any thing shocked or surprised him;—but especially when any thing, which he deemed very absurd, was offered' (I, 21, pp. 92–3). Subsequently,

Sterne then expects us to exercise our awareness of the association of ideas, and to deduce Toby's feelings from his actions. So the whistling of 'Lillabullaro' recurs throughout *Tristram Shandy* whenever Toby is upset; for example when he is waiting with Walter for Tristram's birth, or later on in the novel when he is apprehensive about a meeting with the Widow Wadman.

At times in *Tristram Shandy* Sterne takes external description to extremes. **Would you now read Volume II, Chapter 17, up to the beginning of the sermon (pp. 137–9). What is immediately noticeable about the description of Corporal Trim? What do you think Sterne is trying to convey through this mode of writing?**

## DISCUSSION

What strikes me about this passage is Sterne's almost mathematical precision in describing Trim's stance. I am also struck by the painterly quality of this scene; it's as if Sterne were describing a painter's model rather than a novelist's character.

In this very precise description of Trim's stance, Sterne seems to be conveying his interest in the relationship between external appearance and internal motivation. This kind of presentation of character (i.e. from the outside in) links with Sterne's interest in John Locke's theory of knowledge. Locke is sceptical about the possibility of one person really knowing another, since such knowledge depends on the mutual acceptance of external signs (which include words) to represent experience. Locke wrote:

> Man, though he have a great variety of thoughts, and such from which others as well as himself might receive profit and delight, yet they are all within his own breast, invisible, and hidden from others, nor can themselves be made to appear. The comfort and advantage of society not being to be had without communication of thoughts, it was necessary that man should find some external, visible signs, whereby those invisible ideas might be made known to others.[6]

In Volume II, Chapter 5 of *Tristram Shandy* the narrator has told us what he knows about Trim's character. Here, Sterne is, as it were, testing out Locke's theory in the light of what we already know about Trim. If there is a consensus about the relationship of external signs and a character's intentions, then we can make accurate deductions about that person. Trim stands at an angle of 85 and a half degrees, which, we are told by the narrator, is the angle of stance necessary for persuasion. Therefore, if he stands thus, persuasion should be what he has in mind. In this way, without giving us Trim's thoughts or feelings, Sterne manages to capture precisely his emotions through a

# Characterization

description of his appearance. For example, 'Corporal Trim's eyes and the muscles of his face were in full harmony with the other parts of him;—he looked frank,—unconstrained, something assured, —but not bordering upon assurance' (II, 17, p. 139). This captures very vividly Trim's mixture of deference and confidence, and his awareness of being the centre of attention.

In this chapter Sterne also tries to convey the relationship between form and function, and between art and science. In *Tristram Shandy* Sterne frequently draws on analogies from art for his characterization. In Volume II, Chapter 5, in his description of Trim he has the narrator say 'I have but one stroke to give to finish Corporal Trim's character,—and it is the only dark line in it'.

**Would you now re-read the description of Trim in Volume II, Chapter 17, and pick out the references to painting, drawing and sculpture.**

## DISCUSSION

You will find examples of references to painting, drawing and sculpture in Note 7, in the Endnotes. Did you also include in your list the mention of 'arts and sciences'? These references to visual art recur throughout *Tristram Shandy*. Sterne was a great admirer of William Hogarth (1697-1764) and particularly of his work *The Analysis of Beauty* (1753). Like Sterne, Hogarth was an empiricist. He did not subscribe to the view that beauty has a mathematical basis, but that it is shown in 'fitness'. In other words, beauty is not an ideal compounded of perfect proportions, but is seen when design and use are absolutely fitted to each other. Likewise, Sterne does not give us an ideal character, but sometimes he will give us illustrations of incidents where behaviour is totally appropriate or typical. Sterne was extremely keen for Hogarth to illustrate *Tristram Shandy* because he recognized that Hogarth and he shared a similar philosophy. In a letter written in March 1760, Sterne says '... what would I not give not to have but few strokes of Hogarth's witty chissel at the front of my next Edition of Tristram Shandy ... Now the loosest sketch in nature of Trim's sending the sermon to my father and uncle Toby will content me—'[7]

But as well as the highly visual character of Trim's presentation there is also a sense of parody, as if by his relentless accumulation of detail Sterne is mocking the minute-by-minute realism of a writer such as Richardson. It's almost as if he is saying 'If you want realism, here it is, but don't blame me if you're stifled by so much detail'. A similar kind of attention to exact gesture and attitude occurs in Volume III, Chapter 29. Here is Sterne's description of Walter

Shandy after he learns that Tristram's nose has been crushed at his birth:

> The moment my father got up into his chamber, he threw himself prostrate across his bed in the wildest disorder imaginable, but at the same time, in the most lamentable attitude of a man borne down with sorrows, that ever the eye of pity dropped a tear for.—The palm of his right hand, as he fell upon the bed, receiving his forehead, and covering the greatest part of both his eyes, gently sunk down with his head (his elbow giving way backwards) till his nose touched the quilt;—his left arm hung insensible over the side of the bed, his knuckles reclining upon the handle of the chamber-pot, which peeped out beyond the valance,—his right leg (his left being drawn up towards his body) hung half over the side of the bed, the edge of it pressing upon his shin-bone.—He felt it not. A fixed, inflexible sorrow took possession of every line of his face.—He sighed once,—heaved his breast often,—but uttered not a word. (p. 223)

Sterne has frequently been compared with Samuel Beckett for their similar methods of describing characters by their physical components, and there is no doubt that Beckett's novels owe a debt to Sterne. Here is an extract from Beckett's novel, *Watt*.

> Mr Hackett decided, after some moments, that if they were waiting for a tram they had been doing so for some time. For the lady held the gentleman by the ears, and the gentleman's hand was on the lady's thigh, and the lady's tongue was in the gentleman's mouth. Tired of waiting for the tram, said . . . Mr Hackett, they strike up an acquaintance. The lady now removing her tongue from the gentleman's mouth, he put his into hers. Fair do, said Mr Hackett. Taking a pace forward, to satisfy himself that the gentleman's other hand was not going to waste, Mr Hackett was shocked to find it limply dangling over the back of the seat, with between its fingers the spent three-quarters of a cigarette.[9]

**Would you now compare these passages, which are typical of each author. It might be helpful to identify specifically the words that reinforce the difference between these passages.**

DISCUSSION

I think that the main difference between these extracts is that Sterne, unlike Beckett, gives us adjectives and adverbs which suggest the narrator's empathy with the character, for example: 'wildest', 'lamentable', 'gently', 'insensible', 'fixed', 'inflexible'. Sterne imagines the effect of Walter's posture on an observer who is essentially sympathetic: 'that ever the eye of pity dropped a tear for', and also the effect of Walter's sorrow on himself, which renders him oblivious to the pressures of the bed on his arm and his leg. We have the

# Characterization

detached description of Walter by the narrator, but we also have the narrator's interpretation of his posture, and an imaginative awareness of Walter's physical insensibility brought about by grief. Beckett, on the other hand, pointedly omits any adjectives or adverbs, so that the couple kissing seem devoid of any emotion. He exploits the contrast between the reader's expectations of adjectives such as 'passionately' or 'lovingly' and his stark prose. The episode is funny, because the usually emotional act of kissing is reduced to a mechanical description of the physical interactions necessary to achieve it. It is made funnier by the euphemistic-sounding 'lady' and 'gentleman' which gives them an air of respectability which is then undermined by the implication that they have never met before. This vignette is from the viewpoint of Mr Hackett, who is shocked by it. But his shock is also made amusing, because it is not caused by the inappropriate behaviour of absolute strangers, but because of the waste of resources implied by the man's using one of his two hands to smoke a cigarette.

Sterne, however objective he sets out to be, always imbues his description with feeling. For him, the process of description is didactic. Although he may describe gesture and attitude in great detail, he does so in order to convey the personality of the character he describes. Beckett, on the other hand, depersonalizes his characters by the sustained objectivity of his descriptions. They are reduced to components, devoid of any narratorial sympathy or warmth. Sterne, however, is incapable of withholding an emotional dimension from his characterization, however detached it may appear to be.

**We have looked at Sterne's methods of characterization, but not at the central character of the novel, Tristram Shandy himself. Think about what you know of him. What are the difficulties in assessing his character? Do you see any basic contradiction in what we know about him?**

## DISCUSSION

Perhaps the chief difficulty is that most of the narration is from Tristram Shandy's viewpoint. Therefore we never get an objective view of him from an omniscient narrator, nor even a subjective description of him from the point of view of another character in the novel. All we know about Tristram is what he chooses to reveal to us, and in fact he chooses to tell us very little. We don't know if he's married; we're not told who 'Jenny' is; we're not told of his profession, although he mentions in passing that he owns two 'cassocks' (III, 2) so that we may infer that he is a clergyman. But although the novel is called *The Life and Opinions of Tristram Shandy*, it has not the clarity and cohesion that the title suggests. Tristram's role is twofold: he is both chronicler of his accident-prone childhood, and the central consciousness of his Shandean world, through which we see the differing characters of Walter, Toby, Trim, Dr Slop *et al*. It is as though Tristram seeks to define himself through his descriptions of other people and events. This makes it very difficult to describe him. Henri Fluchère sums up the problem:

> ... he is doubly a literary character, because he is at once the projection of Sterne's mind, and also the dancing-master and teacher of philosophy in the imaginary universe into which he is projected. It is this dual function of circumscribed and stylized literary character —the Shandys' son, humiliated by all sorts of ridiculous little catastrophes—and of universal factotum in the world in which he develops, that makes Tristram a fundamentally ambiguous character.[10]

In other words, the basically simple character of the innocent Tristram is contradicted by the sophistication of the narrator Tristram, who discerns the motivation of other characters, who understands sexual *double entendres*, and who also comprehends Uncle Toby's modesty, which does not permit *him* to understand them. This sophisticated narrator controls the information about the other characters, and also manipulates our attitude towards them. Every incident or character in *Tristram Shandy* is imbued with an explicit or implicit evaluation emanating from Tristram himself, so that our own judgement is also shaped and controlled by him to some extent. By this I mean that, irritating though Uncle Toby might be, I find it impossible to be annoyed with him, since his idiosyncracies are mediated through the narrator's interpretative understanding of them. Similarly, Walter's obsession with philosophy and intellectual theorizing is made palatable by Tristram's repeated assurances of his good nature.

Assessing the character of Tristram Shandy is further complicated by the fact that it is often very difficult to differentiate between Tristram the narrator, and Sterne the author, since their views frequently seem identical. In a letter to David Garrick, Sterne says of *Tristram Shandy* '... 'Tis ... a picture of myself'[11] and this identification extended to his relationship with his characters. And you'll remember in the letter to Richard Berenger asking if it is possible to have Hogarth illustrate *Tristram Shandy*, Sterne says 'The loosest sketch in Nature, of Trim's reading the sermon to my father and my uncle Toby will content me—'. Walter and Toby Shandy thus seem to leap out from the pages of fiction and become Sterne's blood relations. This blurring of fact and fiction is continued by Sterne until his death. He published his sermons under the title *The Sermons of Mr Yorick*, having already included one of them in *Tristram Shandy*. Sometimes, in real life, he signed his letters 'Yorick' and 'Tristram',[12] and in *Tristram Shandy* the narrator is clearly speaking for the author when he talks of the process of writing the novel:

> I would write two volumes every year, provided the vile cough which then tormented me, and which to this hour I dread worse than the devil, would but give me leave . . . I swore it should be kept a-going at that rate these forty years, if it pleased but the fountain of life to bless me so long with health and good spirits.   (VII, 1, p. 459)

Sterne was well aware that the dynamic of *Tristram Shandy* was to a large extent dependent upon this closeness between author and narrator. In a letter to an unknown recipient in 1759, he wrote:

> I will use all reasonable caution—Only with this caution along with it, not to spoil My Book;—that is the air and originality of it, which must resemble the Author—[13]

He is simultaneously aware that in real life he is playing the role he has created for himself. In 1762 he was feted in Paris, and he wrote to David Garrick, 'I Shandy it away fifty times more than I was ever wont . . .'.[14] By 1767, however, he tries to disclaim the identification of Laurence Sterne with Tristram Shandy: 'The world has imagined, because I wrote *Tristram Shandy*, that I was myself more Shandean than I really ever was.'[15] Perhaps his everyday life was not 'Shandean', but there is no doubt that on the publication of the first volumes of *Tristram Shandy* Sterne revelled in the fame they brought him, and acted the parts of Yorick and Tristram almost as if they symbolized qualities that were essentially his. In *Tristram Shandy* Sterne has his hero describe his hobby-horse, having said that the key to a person's character was to find out his hobby-horse, or his ruling passion:

> For my hobby-horse, if you recollect a little, is no way a vicious beast; he has scarce one hair or lineament of the ass about him—'Tis the sporting little filly-folly which carries you out for the present hour—a maggot, a butterfly, a picture, a fiddlestick—an uncle Toby's siege —or an *any thing*, which a man makes a shift to get a-stride on, to canter it away from the cares and solicitudes of life—'Tis as useful a beast as is in the whole creation—nor do I really see how the world could do without it—   (VIII, 31, p. 557)

Incidents, distractions, digressions—these are seen by Sterne not as peripheral, but as important and necessary to escape from the 'cares and solicitudes of life'. His characterization seeks out the quirks, the deviations in people's personalities, the nuances rather than the powerful, monolithic forces or straightforward motivations. Sterne is interested in the atypical, the telling gesture, the eloquent look. He makes us aware that a consistent, logical, purposeful way of behaving may be a façade, and that a true revelation of character lies in the minute observation of the unguarded moment. *Tristram Shandy* is a chronicle of those unguarded moments.

\* \* \*

So far in this chapter it may have appeared that the concept of 'character' employed in the discussion of novels requires no analytic or critical scrutiny. In fact, such analysis is very necessary. The notions of 'character' which open this chapter are shaped and articulated by historical and cultural factors: freedom to cultivate and express individuality, the possibility of determining one's own fate or of being subjected to outside forces, a belief in the individual as knowable—all these contribute to the status given to 'character' both in fiction and in literary criticism. Put simply, in the eighteenth century novelistic characters reflected the confidence and comparative stability of English society. In the eighteenth-century novel, characters seldom change or develop. At the end of the novel they are triumphantly the same, their virtues or vices having been rewarded or punished through the events of the narrative. Their confidence in themselves as consistent is both ratified and justified in the novel. In view of the nineteenth-century emphasis on the importance of 'character' (with its connotations of industriousness, self-discipline and a capacity for self-improvement) it is not surprising that the main criterion for novels and novel criticism was delineation of realistic people. The moral education of characters is a central theme in the nineteenth-century novel, and by the closing chapters they have indeed learnt from their experiences, and are changed by them. Hazlitt (1778–1830), writing about *Tristram Shandy*, praises Sterne for his characterization:

> ... his characters ... are not to be surpassed. It is sufficient to name them;—Yorick, Dr Slop, Mr Shandy, My Uncle Toby, Trim, Susannah, and the Widow Wadman. In these he has contrived to oppose, with equal felicity and originality, two characters, one of pure intellect, and the other of pure good nature, in My Father and My Uncle Toby ... My Father's restlessness, both of body and mind, is inimitable ... My Uncle Toby is one of the finest compliments ever paid to human nature. He is the most unoffending of God's creatures; ... Of his bowling green, his sieges, and his amours, who would say or think anything amiss![16]

Recent critical theory has pointed out that characterization in the novel is no more 'real' than any other narrative strategy, and that it is only what the reader brings to a particular set of signs that reconstructs our concept of character. In other words, we are wrong to attribute more to 'character' in a novel than to any other facet of it, just because we bring qualities of recognition and identification to this aspect of the literary construct.

**Would you now read the following critical extracts, which are about 'character' in fiction. What are the main differences between them? Which most coincides with your view of character in literature?**

1 As for the novelist's characters, they may themselves suggest many possible interpretations; they may, according to the preoccupations of each reader, accommodate all kinds of comment—psychological, psychiatric, religious, or political—yet their indifference to these 'potentialities' will soon be apparent. Whereas the traditional hero is constantly solicited, caught up, destroyed by these interpretations of the author's, ceaselessly projected into an immaterial or unstable *elsewhere*, always more remote and blurred, the future hero will remain, on the contrary, *there*. It is the commentaries that will be left elsewhere; in the face of his irrefutable presence, they will seem useless, superfluous, even improper.[17]  (Alain Robbe-Grillet)

2 When identical semes traverse the same proper name several times and appear to settle on it, a character is created. Thus, the character is a product of combinations: the combination is relatively stable (denoted by the recurrence of the semes) and more or less complex (involving more or less congruent, more or less contradictory figures); this complexity determines the character's 'personality', which is just as much a combination as the odour of a dish or the bouquet of a wine.[18] [A 'seme' in this context means a distinctive unit of meaning.] (Roland Barthes)

3 Fictional characters can possess our imaginations and exploit our memories, which supply us with the evidence of common experience, common humanity... Altering our imaginations, fiction may alter our lives. Novelistic characters in realistic fiction may serve various functions for their creators: spokesmen or targets ... surrogates for forbidden or impossible action ... playthings and puppets ... *alter egos*. Always, though, the novelist has the characters more or less under his conscious or unconscious control. He may claim that his imaginary people take over the action, developing minds of their own. Still, he can always stop writing; without him those people would not exist. As for the reader, once fictional personages enter his imagination they do exist, their power over him greater than his over them. (He can close the book, but the characters survive.)[19]  (Patricia Meyer Spacks)

4 Characters do not exist, are only a collection of instructions, signs or themes. The novel conveys the illusion of subjectivity, but—as we all know in our more rational moments—the novel *only* conveys the illusion ... The ideology of the novel involves as a prerequisite, however, the opposite view that there *are* real

characters in novels who *do* have a kind of provisional reality.[20] (Lennard Davis)

## DISCUSSION

The first two extracts argue for a view of literary character as objective, opaque, irreducible, nonextendible. Robbe-Grillet stresses the irrelevance of interpretation to the *Dinglichkeit*—the thing-ness—of characters, who will remain intrinsically and inseparably part of the novel's structure. Barthes, by analysing the construction of character in linguistic terms, is making a similar point. Character is the result of a linguistic process, no more, no less, and thus complexity of character is the result of a complex use of language. He goes on to say later in *S/Z* that

> the person is no more than a collection of semes ... What gives the illusion that the sum is supplemented by a precious remainder (something like *individuality*, in that, qualitative and ineffable, it may escape the vulgar bookkeeping of compositional characters) is the Proper Name, the difference completed by what is *proper* to it. The proper name enables the person to exist outside the semes, whose sum nonetheless constitutes it entirely. (p. 191)

The third extract imbues fictional characters not only with personalities, but with influence over the reader. There is no question here of the character being seen *merely* as a construct of linguistic units. For Meyer Spacks, the characters not only take on a life of their own ('He can close the book, but the characters survive'), but they are also powerful therapists, almost, for the reader. This is an opposite viewpoint to that of the first two extracts.

In the final piece, Lennard Davis encapsulates both points of view: the awareness that characters in fiction are in fact words on a page, but that the ideology of the novel necessitates our belief, simultaneously and paradoxically, in the temporary reality of its characters. So, I would see the Robbe-Grillet and the Barthes extracts as similar, differing profoundly from Patricia Meyer Spacks, and finally Lennard Davis summarizing very succinctly their differences, and the precise difficulty we're up against. That is, *of course* a novel is composed of words, and a character in a novel is composed of words just as the description of a motorcar or a dining room is composed of words. Nevertheless, neither an author nor a reader can confront words in total innocence, and certain words have emotive or evaluative connotations which are very difficult to dislodge. The associations adhering to a particular word may differ between writer and reader, but what cannot be achieved, as we saw in the previous chapter of this *Guide*, is pure neutrality. Words come contaminated, sticky with usage in real situations, and characterization sometimes relies quite heavily on the anticipated reader's response to selected words. So, I suggest that the problem of literary criticism in relation to the realistic representation of character is one of balance. On one hand, we need to acknowledge that characters in novels are not simply snapshots, as it were, of real people, but painstaking and complex linguistic creations. On the other hand, I think we need to recognize that both readers and authors bring to characters identifications and recognitions from real life. So, to use Barthes' expression positively rather than negatively, there *is* a 'precious remainder', which is the relationship between the author, the reader and the words on the page. And the links in this relationship are those of real, everyday experience from which characters derive, and to which they return through the phenomenon of being read and interpreted by a real person.

This is a complex and fascinating subject, which we cannot pursue at further length here, but the key point to keep in mind is the linguistic basis of any concept of 'character' in the novel. If you want to explore the problem further, you could consult the critics quoted above, and also the titles mentioned under Further Reading.

# 5. Reflexive

A 'reflexive' novel is one that draws attention to its own form. In contrast, a 'realist' novel makes every attempt to divert attention from its formal qualities in order to convince you of the veracity of the narrative. *Tristram Shandy* clearly comes into the first category.

**Would you now list the principal ways in which Sterne draws attention to the formal aspects of the novel (some of which we've already looked at).**

DISCUSSION

Sterne's use of typographical devices reinforces our awareness of the book as a physical object, thereby sabotaging our belief in the narrative as a 'real' world. His constant references to the process of writing the novel have a similar effect; we are distracted from the plot to the author's/narrator's formal problems in writing it. The techniques of constructing a chronological narrative give him great trouble, and there are several explanations and justifications for the numerous digressions. The relationship of time in the novel with time outside it alarms and mystifies the narrator: his readers are not allowed to 'lose' themselves in the time scale of the novel without being reminded of its artificiality. And, as we saw in Chapter 3 of the *Guide*, the intrusive narrator makes constant reference to the reader and the act of reading, thereby reminding us that we are engaging with a fictional world, and drawing attention to the fictiveness of the novel.

We have already looked at Sterne's use of the reader in *Tristram Shandy*, and in the next chapter of this *Guide* I shall concentrate on Sterne's interest in time and narrative order. Here I want to focus on his other reflexive devices: the typography of *Tristram Shandy* and the narrator's running commentary on the difficulties of writing a novel.

Perhaps the most obvious typographical device in *Tristram Shandy* is the use of the dash. It is Sterne's hallmark, and its purpose seems to vary. Sometimes it is used instead of a full stop, or as parenthesis. Sometimes it indicates flow where a full stop would create too much of a pause. Most often it is used as a dynamic gesture which enacts the uninhibited rush of the thought process. One idea follows another, exemplifying or contradicting the first, and often the dashes represent breathlessness, as if the narrator were almost overcome by the speed at which his ideas are brought to consciousness. William V. Holtz has tried the experiment of conventionally repunctuating a passage from *Tristram Shandy* and comparing it with the original. For example:

| | |
|---|---|
| For as soon as my father had done insulting his HOBBY-HORSE,—he turned his head without the least emotion, from Dr Slop, to whom he was addressing his discourse, and looked up into my father's face, with a countenance spread over with so much good nature:— so placid;—so fraternal;—so inexpressibly tender towards him;—it penetrated my father | For as soon as my father had done insulting his HOBBY-HORSE, he turned his head without the least emotion, from Dr Slop, to whom he was addressing his discourse, and looked up into my father's face, with a countenance spread over with so much good nature, so placid, so fraternal, so inexpressibly tender towards him it penetrated my father |

*Reflexive*

| | |
|---|---|
| to his heart: He rose up hastily from his chair, and seizing hold of both my uncle Toby's hands as he spoke:—Brother Toby, said he,—I beg thy pardon; —forgive, I pray thee, this rash humour which my mother gave me.   (II, 12, p. 132) | to his heart: He rose up hastily from his chair, and seizing hold of both my uncle Toby's hands as he spoke: 'Brother Toby,' said he, 'I beg thy pardon; —forgive, I pray thee, this rash humour which my mother gave me.' |

**What would you say is the difference in effect between the two?**

DISCUSSION

The first dash suggests quite a long pause, or even the actual trajectory of Toby's head movement. The substitute comma simply indicates a brief pause, and a slight change of topic. The next three dashes after 'nature', 'placid' and 'fraternal' again suggest long pauses, and thus give emphasis to the words before them. We linger on each virtue before going on to the next one described. The substitute commas merely separate a list. The dash after 'him' indicates a dramatic pause. Will Walter Shandy respond or not? It also appears to me (although I admit this is fanciful) that it almost illustrates the penetrating qualities of Toby's look which, in metaphorical terms, turns into an arrow which 'penetrated my father to his heart'. The lack of punctuation in the amended version takes away the suspense and makes Walter Shandy's repentance seem more inevitable. The final three dashes indicate Walter's halting speech, and make him sound more sincere and less fluent than in the amended version. Thus I am arguing that the dashes are eloquent, rather than silent. Their lengths allow the reader to pause, and sometimes to feed in meaning which may be implied, but is not stated. Their use enlivens the text, makes it nearer conversation and further from writing. Conventional punctuation is a literary device which reinforces our sense of the written words, the written sentence. The comma or full stop merely breaks up the flow of words. It does not usually add meaning in the way that Sterne's dashes enhance or complement the words between them.

If you think my reading of the dashes is allowing them too much significance, try Holtz's exercise for yourself. Rewrite a paragraph or so with conventional punctuation, and note the different effect it has on your reading of that particular passage. Possible extracts might be Volume VII, Chapter 2, the paragraph about seasickness: 'When shall we get to land? . . . what's the matter?' (p. 461); or the episode of Corporal Trim and the Beguine (VIII, 22), from 'The young Beguine . . . madest a speech' (pp. 548–9).

Sterne exploits various types of print in order to give emphases to his text. Italics and upper-case characters are frequently used, as is Gothic script in Mrs Shandy's marriage settlement (I, 15, pp. 65–9) in order to underline its legal nature. The potential of typography allows Sterne to play games with the reader, as, for example, in Volume VI, Chapter 11, where he has Yorick write 'Bravo!' at the end of one of his sermons. The narrator then says

> ... I am aware that, in publishing this, I do no service to Yorick's character as a modest man;—but all men have their failings! and what lessens this still farther, and almost wipes it away, is this; that the word was struck through some time afterwards (as appears from a different tint of the ink) with a line quite across it in this manner, ~~BRAVO~~ ——as if he had retracted, or was ashamed of the opinion he had once entertained of it. (VI, 11, p. 415)

**How does that typographical oddity affect your reading of that passage?**

## DISCUSSION

The process of ordinary reading is the interpretation of signs. A noun, for example, signifies a concept which, by convention, we accept as its 'meaning'. While we read we are unconsciously engaged in a process of translation. When Sterne explains that Yorick subsequently deletes his somewhat vain comment, he puts it like this: 'the word was struck through some time afterwards (as appears from a different tint of the ink) with a line quite across it ...' If we read that, we are aware of the slightly archaic language ('struck through' instead of 'crossed out') but we are able to use our imaginations to envisage the crossed-out word. But suddenly Sterne writes: 'in this manner', and actually illustrates in front of our eyes what was previously left for us to imagine. In fact, during our actual reading of the preceding line, the word stands out at us; we are being *shown* something directly, and this subverts the reading process which, as I have suggested, is one of interpretation. The immediacy of the illustration makes the description of it redundant. The crossed-out 'bravo' is interesting also in that the line across it does not cancel out the word completely, so that like shot silk, its positive meaning seems almost to alternate with its negation. Or perhaps it would be more accurate to say that both meanings, positive and negative, are there simultaneously. The line does not totally fulfil its nullifying function; just as when in court a judge asks the jury to ignore a certain statement, the words do not totally obliterate that statement from their minds, rather the reverse.

\* \* \*

On picking up a novel to read, we expect to be confronted with written words arranged in lines to be read (in European culture, at least) from left to right. When words give way to drawings, or black, mottled or blank pages, there is some feeling of shock, of the 'rules' having been violated. The withholding of words from a reader is a subversive action. It thwarts our expectations, and forces us to seek meaning in the absence of words. As we saw in Chapter 1 of this *Guide*, the black pages after Yorick's death invoke a period of mourning, of decent silence, almost as if both writer and reader are too upset to cope with the nuances of language immediately after taking in the fact of his death. The marbled pages (III, 36, pp. 233–4) are offered as an emblem of the variety and complexity of *Tristram Shandy* itself: 'motley symbol of all my work'. 'Motley' is the name for the traditional jester's costume, and in making the comparison Sterne seems to be mocking the reader's desire to make sense of the novel. The marbled pages cannot be interpreted; however much we gaze at them they remain random, persistently chaotic. In *Tristram Shandy* Sterne is concerned with *not* reducing complexity to the simplicity of realism. It's almost as if words are too intelligible, too 'translatable' for him to use all the time, so that the swirling chaos of the marbled page becomes more nearly a representation of what Sterne wants to convey.

Conventionally, pages are to be filled with words by the author. Sterne's sense of the book's physicality allows him to leave pages blank, or to pretend that he's torn a page out altogether (I, 25, p. 101). In Volume IV he omits a whole chapter, so that there is no Chapter 24, and the pagination (in the Penguin edition) goes from p. 300 to p. 311: 'a chasm of ten pages made in the book' (IV, 25). In the following chapter the narrator proceeds to tell the reader the contents of the missing chapter, which has been 'omitted' because it is stylistically inconsistent with the rest of the novel. Sterne continues his subversion of literary expectations by the introduction of line drawings, used instead of words. In the famous passage in Volume IX, Chapter 4, he discards words as too inflexible to convey what he needs to express. Corporal Trim is talking of freedom: 'When a man is free,—cried the corporal, giving a flourish with his stick thus—' (p. 576). A twirling line appears on the page (reproduced on the cover of this guide), after which the narrator notes: 'A thousand of my father's most subtle syllogisms could not have said more for celibacy' (IX, 4). Both the graphic illustration, and the succeeding sentence emphasize Sterne's acute awareness of the limitations of words. What he wants to convey is a feeling of fluidity, and in using a swirling, wavy line running down the page he achieves it in two senses: first by the abandon the line expresses visually to the reader,

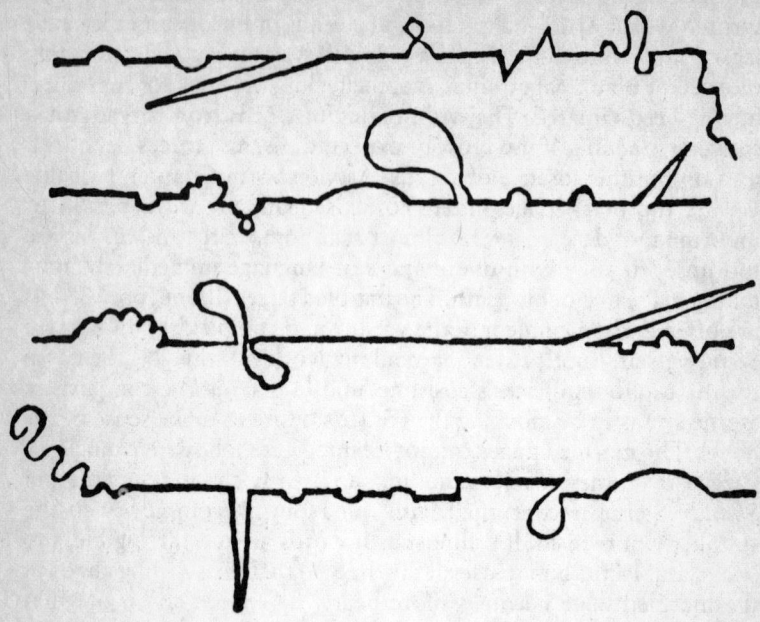

4   Graph from *Tristram Shandy* showing narrative lines

and second, by the ease and freedom with which he jettisons language as and when he wants. The drawing both illustrates and enacts its message.

In order to illustrate the line of the narrative in *Tristram Shandy* Sterne draws four wiggly lines to demonstrate both the progress and the digression of his plot in Volumes II, III, IV and V (VI, 40, p. 453) (see illustration 4). These are not drawings relating to the content of the novel, but rather to its actual structure. The reader's attention is brought to the theory of fiction; we are made to look at the difficulties inherent in narrative progression. How do you keep your narrative moving forward when digression continually halts its progress? Again, and I cannot stress this too much, Sterne's tactics are the opposite of a realist writer's: he is deliberately foregrounding the technical aspects of novel-writing, and this foregrounding inevitably weakens our belief in the novel's plot and characters. And yet, paradoxically, the tactic of using line drawings, for example, enhances and widens our involvement with the novel, since it then extends to the problems of the author/narrator. We are included in the creative process. We become privileged confidants. We are shown the complicated mechanism needed to render reality into fiction, instead of merely being presented with the glossy, apparently seamless, finished object.

These reflexive techniques insist that the reader acknowledge the novel as a physical object, as well as an imagined world. Throughout *Tristram Shandy* there is a powerful tension between the book-as-object and the book-as-narration, and this tension is carefully maintained by Sterne. Every so often, at various points where the reader is in danger of submitting to the power of the narrative, a reflexive device jerks us out of the comfortable feeling of gradually becoming 'lost' in a novel. We are abrasively reminded of the act of reading and our role as readers, and that the book has covers and pages.

**Would you now reread Volume III, Chapter 31. Concentrate especially on the following lines:**

> —Here are two senses, cried Eugenius, as we walked along, pointing with the fore finger of his right hand to the word *Crevice*, in the fifty-second page of the second volume of this book of books.—— here are two senses,—quoth he.—And here are two roads, replied I, turning short upon him,—a dirty and a clean one,—which shall we take?—The clean,——by all means, replied Eugenius. (III, 31, p. 225)

**What is strange about this extract, and how does it relate to Sterne's view of the novel form?**

## DISCUSSION

The strange thing about this passage is that Eugenius and Tristram, characters within the novel *Tristram Shandy*, are referring to an earlier page of the novel they're in: 'the fifty-second page of the second volume of this book of books'. They are discussing the *double entendre* implicit in the word 'crevice' as used in Volume II, Chapter 7 (pp. 121–2), and which we have already looked at (p. 39).

Sterne's view of the novel form is unusual in that he considers the form itself the main subject of his novel. For Eugenius and Tristram to be talking about a word in the novel *Tristram Shandy* would seem entirely appropriate subject matter, since Tristram as narrator is perpetually concerned with the act of writing. This reflexivity extends to the discussion of technical problems inherent in writing a novel.

A notable instance of these problems is the difficulty of moving characters from place to place. Consider the following examples:

> 1 Dr Slop drew up his mouth, and was just beginning to return my uncle Toby the compliment of his Whu—u—u— or interjectional whistle,—when the door hastily opening in the next chapter but one—put an end to the affair.   (III, 11, p. 191)

The effect of this is surreal: 'realism' and 'reflexivity' clash as the ordinariness of 'the door opening' is juxtaposed with the words 'in the next chapter' as if the chapter were a physical place. The effect is confusing, since our allegiance to realism (belief in 'the door') is totally undercut by the reflexive reference to its being a fiction, merely a construct of words which occurs 'in the next chapter'. Sterne plays these games all the time, but usually a piece of realism is interspersed with a comment about the physical aspects of a book, or the techniques of writing. Here the two are used in the course of a single sentence, indeed, in a subordinate clause, and the result is audacious.

> 2 Is it not a shame to make two chapters of what passed in going down one pair of stairs? for we are got no farther yet than to the first landing, and there are fifteen more steps down to the bottom; and for aught I know, as my father and my uncle Toby are in a talking humour, there may be as many chapters as steps;—let that be as it will, Sir, I can no more help it than my destiny:—A sudden impulse comes across me—drop the curtain, Shandy—I drop it—Strike a line here across the paper, Tristram—I strike it—and hey for a new chapter!   (IV, 10, p. 282)

This passage makes extraordinary suppositions about the relationship between characters and narrator, and narrator and author. The narrator speaks of the characters as if they have power over the narrative. If they decide to talk a lot, then this will necessitate several chapters, as if the author's task is merely to transcribe their conversation. The characters here seem to dictate the format of the novel, rather than *vice versa*. And there is in this passage the further confusion in the last few lines. Is the narrator talking to himself in the third person—'drop the curtain, Shandy'—or is the 'me' figure a super-narrator, the voice, as it were, of Sterne himself, telling Tristram what to do?

> 3 HOLLA!—you chairman!—here's sixpence—do step into that bookseller's shop, and call me a *day-tall* critic. I am very willing to give any one of 'em a crown to help me with his tackling, to get my father and my uncle Toby off the stairs, and to put them to bed.——
> [. . .]

> —So then, friend! you have got my father and my uncle Toby off the stairs, and seen them to bed?——And how did you manage it?—You dropped a curtain at the stairs foot—I thought you had no other way for it——Here's a crown for your trouble.   (IV, 13, pp. 285–7)
> ['Day-tall' means paid by the day.]

Here, engagingly, the narrator offers a freelance critic the task of getting these fictional characters off the stairs and to bed. The narrator then makes a long observation about the problems of infinite regression in writing *Tristram Shandy*, and at the end of the chapter returns, as it were, to see how the critic has got on. He then pays him for his help! In one way this episode emphasizes the fictiveness of *Tristram Shandy*: it contains characters that can be manipulated, moved around like cardboard figures, even by outsiders. But in another way, this manoeuvre makes Tristram himself seem more realistic, rather than less. In comparison with Walter and Toby Shandy, Tristram appears to be non-fictional, or at least *less* fictional than the other characters. All this is an illusion, of course. Tristram, Walter and Toby Shandy have exactly the same fictive status. But Tristram always seems more than just another fictional character, partly because all the other characters are seen from his point of view, and partly because his problems with writing the narrative are foregrounded. There are numerous other examples of this kind, which you might like to find for yourself. They all illustrate the relexive nature of *Tristram Shandy*. Do you see how different it is from a conventional realist novel, where the author perpetually keeps the reader involved in the plot, as if there were no technical problems to be overcome? We may begin this novel hoping to learn about the life and opinions of Tristram Shandy, Gent., and in this we will be frustrated. But we will almost certainly end it knowing far more about the theory of the novel form in general.

*  *  *

The structure of Tristram Shandy reveals its digressive nature. If I asked you to draw a diagram of the structure of a typical realist novel, you would probably find it very easy. There might be some flashbacks, some digressions, but overall the movement of the plot would be progressive and mostly undeviating. A diagram of the structure of *Tristram Shandy* would be more challenging, to say the least. Sterne's diagrams in Volume VI, Chapter 40 contain a great many loops and curves, indicating the complexity of the plot, and the impossibility of delineating it as one of steady progression.

**Would you now look at the following extracts.**

1 What can they be doing, brother?—quoth my father,—we can scarce hear ourselves talk.

   I think, replied my uncle Toby, taking his pipe from his mouth, and striking the head of it two or three times upon the nail of his left thumb, as he began his sentence,——I think, says he:——But to enter rightly into my uncle Toby's sentiments upon this matter, you must be made to enter a little into his character, the outlines of which I shall just give you, and then the dialogue between him and my father shall go on as well again. (I, 21, p. 87)

2 My mother was going very gingerly in the dark along the passage which led to the parlour, as my uncle Toby pronounced the word *wife*.—'Tis a shrill penetrating sound of itself, and Obadiah had helped it by leaving the door a little ajar, so that my mother heard enough of it, to imagine herself the subject of the conversation: so laying the edge of her finger across her two lips—holding in her breath, and bending her head a little downwards, with a twist of her neck—(not towards the door, but from it, by which means her ear was brought to the chink)—she listened with all her powers:—the listening slave, with the Goddess of Silence at his back, could not have given a finer thought for an intaglio [gem with incised design].

   In this attitude I am determined to let her stand for five minutes: till I bring up the affairs of the kitchen (as Rapin does those of the church) to the same period. (V, 5, pp. 352–3)

In each case Sterne abandons these episodes for a while.

**Where in the novel are they picked up again, what has occupied the narrator in between and what effect does this have on the narrative?**

## DISCUSSION

The first extract is continued in Volume II, Chapter 6 (pp. 118–9):

> What can they be doing, brother? said my father.—I think, replied my uncle Toby,—taking, as I told you, his pipe from his mouth, and striking the ashes out of it as he began his sentence; ——I think, replied he,—it would not be amiss, brother, if we rung the bell.

The second extract is continued in Volume V, Chapter 12 (p. 362): 'But to return to my mother'. The effect on the narrative is to slow down the pace, and to undermine the element of suspense. This may sound paradoxical, because a digression in the middle of Tristram's birth should increase our suspense, rather than diminish it. But I suggest that by the time the narrator returns to the theme of Mrs Shandy's confinement, we've almost forgotten about it. The digression lasts for thirty pages, and deals in detail with Aunt Dinah's misalliance with the coachman, and the modesty of Uncle Toby's character (Ch. 21). It then includes a long defence of digression (Ch.

22), a dissertation on the difficulties of characterization (Ch. 23), the uniqueness of uncle Toby's 'hobby-horse' (Ch. 24), a description of his life after his wound at Namur (Ch. 25 and Volume II, Ch. 1), an invitation and address to critics (Ch. 2), Uncle Toby's recovery, researches into ballistics and his relationship with Corporal Trim (Chs. 3, 4 and 5). The second digression is shorter, but it covers the topics of communication in the Shandy household, the announcement of Bobby's death and the servants' reactions to it (Ch. 7), talk about a chapter on 'chamber-maids' and 'button-holes' (Ch. 8), Trim's speech (Ch. 9), the servants' conjecture about the Shandys' reactions to the tragedy (Ch. 10), and the narrator's thoughts on his judgement (Ch. 11). Again, it slows down the pace of the main plot, but makes us realize, surely, that the digressions also diminish the importance of the central narrative. For the news of Bobby Shandy's death is obviously substantial, and so is the information about the character of Uncle Toby. Sterne does not seem to allocate significant events only to the main plot, nor does he leave only trivia for his digressions. Not surprisingly, throughout *Tristram Shandy* he defends the practice of deviating from his plot.

The implications of Sterne's defence of digression are wide-reaching. He is saying, in effect, that 'it is better to travel than to arrive', and there is a strong moral bias towards the person who has 'fifty deviations from a straight line to make with this or that party as he goes along' (I, 14, p. 64). This philosophy is central to our understanding of *Tristram Shandy*. Sterne is for variety, divergence, involvement. His narrator is happily seduced hither and thither, and everything is grist to his mill. Single-mindedness and convergence are not qualities Sterne would have admired. In Volume VIII he says

> I defy the best cabbage planter ... to go on coolly, critically, and canonically, planting his cabbages one by one, in straight lines, and stoical distances, especially if slits in petticoats are unsewed up—without ever and anon straddling out, or sidling into some bastardly digression. (VIII, 1, p. 515)

Indeed, he suggests that the ability to allow oneself to digress in a novel and in real life is a method of enriching and enlivening the periods of either which are potentially flat and boring:

> How far my pen has been fatigued like those of other travellers, in this journey of it, over so barren a track—the world must judge—but the traces of it, which are now all set o' vibrating together this moment, tell me 'tis the most fruitful and busy period of my life; for as I had made no convention with my man with the gun as to time—by stopping and talking to every soul I met who was not in a full trot—joining all parties before me—waiting for every soul behind —hailing all those who were coming through cross-roads—arresting

> all kinds of beggars, pilgrims, fiddlers, friars—not passing by a woman in a mulberry-tree without commending her legs, and tempting her into conversation with a pinch of snuff——In short, by seizing every handle, of what size or shape soever, which chance held out to me in this journey—I turned my *plain* into a *city*— (VII, 43, pp. 510–11)

Thus digressions transform *Tristram Shandy*. What might have been a straightforward journey becomes a confusing, complex and rich experience—so much so that most of us give up our expectations of 'getting anywhere' with the narrative in a conventional sense. But the act of giving up the idea of progress is, paradoxically, the beginning of getting somewhere. It's just that by accepting Sterne's redefinitions, by making digression central rather than peripheral, we are forced to change the nature of our goals.

Sterne, as I mentioned in Chapter 4, was a great admirer of Hogarth. Here are two quotations from Hogarth's book on the theory of art, *The Analysis of Beauty*. As you read them, would you compare his theory with Sterne's on digression, and see how closely they relate to each other.

> Intricacy in form, therefore, I shall define to be that peculiarity in the lines which compose it, that *leads the eye a wanton kind of chase*, and from the pleasure that gives the mind, entitles it to the name of beautiful.[2]

> And that the serpentine line, by its waving and winding at the same time different ways, leads the eye in a pleasing manner along the continuity of its variety, if I may be allowed the expression; and which by its twisting so many different ways, may be said to include (tho' but a single line) varied contents; and therefore all its variety cannot be expressed on paper by one continued line, without the assistance of the imagination.[3]

## DISCUSSION

Clearly, Sterne and Hogarth have very similar views on narrative and artistic lines. Indeed, 'a wanton kind of chase' could be used as a very apt description of the narrative method of *Tristram Shandy* as a whole. In this first quotation Hogarth seems to be saying that the beauty of form is not intrinsic, but is derived from the 'pleasure it gives the mind'. In other words, the final beauty is a combination of both artistic form and the viewer's response to it. This links with Sterne's insistence on the reader's involvement with his novel: 'The truest respect which you can pay to the reader's understanding, is to halve this matter amicably, and leave him something to imagine, in his turn, as well as yourself' (II, 11, p. 127). Both artists see virtue and beauty in digression from the perfectly straight line, and Hogarth's expression 'the continuity of its variety' relates to the apparent paradox employed by Sterne when he talks about the 'two contrary motions' which are 'introduced . . . and reconciled' (I, 22, p. 95). In their respective works, Sterne and Hogarth seek to combine both stasis and progression. Although working in a spatial medium, Hogarth was famous for his 'narrative' paintings, which show a temporal sequence of events, such as *A Harlot's Progress* and *A Rake's Progress*. One picture leads in chronological order to another. Instead of depicting merely one frozen moment in time, Hogarth implies a progression, a movement, by a series of sequential pictures. In this way he makes a plot, with characters and a beginning, a middle and an end. Pictorial art thus merges with narrative fiction.

Sterne, conversely, attempts to transcend what he sees as the limitations of narrative by 'freezing' his characters so that instead of appearing to progress, the effect is both static and spatial. 'Let me stop and give you a picture . . .' says Tristram (VI, 25, p. 435). So characters are drawn with what seems an almost absurd emphasis on detail: Walter sprawled in despair upon his bed, Corporal Trim poised to read the sermon, Mrs Shandy listening at the door. Characters are often frozen in positions, suspended, as it were, in mid-chapter, as if the frame of a film has been frozen for us to examine it outside its narrative context. Hogarth's phrase 'the continuity of its variety' could easily refer to the narrative line in *Tristram Shandy*. It varies between progression, digression and stasis, and by its 'twisting' in itself expresses Sterne's dissatisfaction with 'one continued line.' Such a line is inadequate, Sterne implies, not only artistically, but morally. The whole of *Tristram Shandy* is an argument in favour of the various rather than the singular, the serpentine line rather than the straight. Sterne talks about this several times in figurative terms, referring to motion versus stasis (I, 22), the straight versus the curvaceous line (VI, 40), the plain versus the city (VII, 43).

For Sterne, the quality of the journey is more important than the actual arrival, and it is not surprising that in *Tristram Shandy* several stories are begun and not completed. Walter Shandy's *Tristrapaedia*, the story of Aunt Dinah and the coachman, and the tale of the King of Bohemia, all remain unfinished.

> . . . Bohemia! said my uncle Toby – – – – musing a long time – – –
> What became of that story, Trim?
>     —We lost it, an' please your honour, somehow betwixt us.  (VIII, 28, p. 554)

says Trim, and this conversation is emblematic of the novel as a whole. Tristram, the narrator, is trying to tell a story to us, his readers. The story never really gets off the ground, and it tails off abruptly: 'We lost it... somehow betwixt us'. Sterne's insistence on the reflexivity of his text contributes to the loss of the 'story'. It also makes clear that he did not believe in the possibility of completion in the first place, since all his comments on writing undermine the notion of arrival, of neat and tidy endings. If you look at *Tristram Shandy* as an illustration of a *process*, the process of trying to write a novel, it will make much more sense than if you see it as an uncompleted story.

\* \* \*

In the nineteenth century, criticism of *Tristram Shandy* was confined mainly to admiration of his characterization and condemnation of his bawdiness. It was not until the twentieth century that the reflexive nature of this novel was first appreciated, and subsequent criticism has usually concentrated on the formal aspects of it. The Modernist movement (spanning the late nineteenth and early twentieth centuries) shared many of the reflexive interests expressed artistically by Sterne, and it is not surprising that a writer such as Virginia Woolf greatly admired him. Indeed, he has often been called the first Modernist, or used as an example to disprove the novelty of the Modernist movement in literature. For all their achievements, such writers as Proust, Joyce, Mann, and Woolf, and later Beckett and Nabokov, do not attempt anything that had not been prefigured by Laurence Sterne. They may elaborate, their angles and emphases may lie differently, but he has been there before them, and any adequate assessment of Modernism needs to begin by acknowledging the great legacy of *Tristram Shandy*, published between 1760 and 1767.

The first and highly important article on Sterne as a reflexive writer was written in 1921 by a Russian critic called Victor Shklovsky (1893–1984). He was a member of a group of critics called the Russian Formalists, who emphasized the importance of artistic technique, rather than that of content. Shklovsky's effect on twentieth-century literary criticism has been extremely influential. Indeed, Terry Eagleton begins his book *Literary Theory* like this:

> If one wanted to put a date on the beginnings of the transformation which has overtaken literary theory in this century, one could do worse than settle on 1917, the year in which the young Russian Formalist Victor Shklovsky published his pioneering essay 'Art as Device'.[4]

The Russian Formalists, who included Roman Jakobson, had a powerful influence on the French structuralist movement later this century. Here is an extract from Shklovsky's 1917 essay, the title of which is variously translated as 'Art as Device' or 'Art as Technique'. What is he saying, and how does it link with the reflexive nature of *Tristram Shandy*?

> Habitualization devours works, clothes, furniture, one's wife, and the fear of war. 'If the whole complex lives of many people go on unconsciously, then such lives are as if they had never been'. [Extract from Tolstoy's diary, 1 March, 1897.] And art exists that one may recover the sensation of life; it exists to make one feel things, to make the stone *stony*. The purpose of art is to impart the sensation of things as they are perceived and not as they are known. The technique of art is to make objects 'unfamiliar', to make forms difficult, to increase the difficulty and length of perception because the process of perception is an aesthetic end in itself and must be prolonged. *Art is a way of experiencing the artfulness of an object; the object is not important.*[5]

**What is Shklovsky's argument here, and how does it apply to *Tristram Shandy*?**

DISCUSSION

Shklovsky is saying that habitual ways of seeing negate all kinds of experience. The quotation from Tolstoy reinforces this: if we go about our lives without awareness, it's almost as if we haven't existed. Shklovsky goes on to say that art exists so that we can rediscover a freshness of perception, to sharpen our sensations of reality. He says that the purpose of art is to give us back the immediacy of feeling involved in perception, not the feeling of things as we already know them. Thus, the technique of art is to make familiar objects seem strange (in order to enable us to 'see' them afresh), to make formal aspects of art difficult so as to increase the time it takes us to perceive something. This attempt to prolong (through difficulty) the process of perception is important because this process is an end in itself, not merely a means to an end. Art is a way by which we are enabled to experience the *un*reality of an object, its strangeness. The actual object is unimportant compared with our 'retraining' in the ways of perceiving. How does Shklovsky's view of art link with the reflexive nature of *Tristram Shandy*? Throughout his book Sterne disturbs our habitual assumptions about the function of a novel. If we go to *Tristram Shandy* with 'realist' expectations that the language will be transparent—merely there to convey a 'content'—we are likely to be startled, to say the least. As we have seen, Sterne constantly puts obstacles in the way of our accustomed process of reading: typographical devices; references to the difficulties of writing; demands that the reader fill in gaps with words or with drawings, transposing information so that cause follows effect; digressions and theories about them; and so on. Our desire to become immersed in the story (which corresponds to Shklovsky's 'object') is thwarted by Sterne's insistence on our awareness of the process: 'a way of experiencing the artfulness of an object'. The story line is subordinated again and again to an exploration and rejection of the techniques of realism. It should make us begin to wonder how in fact a realist novelist *does* get someone off the stairs, how the problem is dealt with, how adequate are the realist methods of characterization. Sterne makes the book, *booky*, if you like. Our attention is drawn to its physicality, and to the techniques of fiction. It is impossible to finish reading *Tristram Shandy*, I suggest, without a heightened awareness of the 'artfulness' of a novelist, whether realist or not, and of the conventions that we, as readers, habitually accept and employ when reading a novel.

In 1921 Shklovsky published what he called a 'stylistic commentary' on *Tristram Shandy*, having noted that 'nothing much is written about Sterne any more; or, if it is, it consists only of a few banalities'. From his earlier essay it is easy to see why he was so attracted to this novel. He says, 'Formalistically, Sterne was a great revolutionary; it was characteristic of him to "lay bare" his technique'.[6] Shklovsky is particularly interested in Sterne's games with time (which we look at in the next chapter) and with what he calls 'erotic defamiliarization'. In 'Art as Technique' he says that 'Art removes objects from the automatism of perception in several ways', one of which is to make the familiar strange by various methods. He says that 'Tolstoy makes the familiar seem strange by not naming the familiar object', and quotes an example where flogging is defined by Tolstoy: 'to strip people who have broken the law, to hurl them to the floor, and to rap on their bottoms with sticks'. This defamiliarization comes through an objective description of a process which does not allow the reader to experience whatever automatic connotations the word 'flogging' brings to mind.

Sterne, suggests Shklovsky, employs a similar process, often using elaborate euphemism to avoid specific naming, particularly with regard to sexuality. Shklovsky quotes the example of the hot chestnut in Phutatorius' breeches:

> Now whether it was physically impossible, with half a dozen hands all thrust into the napkin at a time—but that some one chestnut, of more life and rotundity than the rest, must be put in motion—it so fell out, however, that one was actually sent rolling off the table; and as Phutatorius sat straddling under—it fell perpendicularly into that particular aperture of Phutatorius's breeches, for which, to the shame and indelicacy of our language be it spoke, there is no chaste word

throughout all Johnson's dictionary—let it suffice to say—it was that particular aperture, which in all good societies, the laws of decorum do strictly require, like the temple of Janus (in peace at least) to be universally shut up. (IV, 27, p. 317)

This euphemistic avoidance of the sexually obvious runs through *Tristram Shandy*, from the episode of *coitus interruptus* at the very beginning of the novel. The 'naming of parts' is precisely what Sterne refuses to do, and his methods of circumvention distract our attention from the narrative to his way of narrating it. But having created an obstacle to our immediate perception, our final understanding is thereby enhanced and enlivened in a way that would not have been achieved had the story been told straightforwardly. When we finally realize the absurd situation of Tristram's conception, or the exact destination of the hot chestnut, the incident is far funnier, far wittier than it would have been without 'erotic defamiliarization'.

In his essay on Sterne, Shklovsky offers one of the best descriptions of what *Tristram Shandy* is about. 'By violating the form, he forces us to attend to it; and, for him, this awareness of the form through its violation constitutes the content of the novel.'[7] It could be called the archetypal example of reflexive fiction, and writers such as James Joyce and Samuel Beckett owe a great debt to Sterne. It is the first great 'anti-novel', and an anti-novel can exist only in opposition to a novel. *Tristram Shandy* is based on a palimpsest of a realist text. It breaks all the rules of realism, and yet, in an ultimate paradox, depends for its effect on the reader's constant awareness of those rules. The process of defamiliarization can only work with what is already familiar to the reader, and it is this apparent contradiction that Sterne so skilfully exploits.

# 6. Time

In the previous chapter we looked at some of the devices Sterne uses in *Tristram Shandy* to draw attention to its form. In this final chapter of the *Guide* I want to tackle what is perhaps the most difficult aspect of *Tristram Shandy*: Sterne's attitude to time within the novel. You will not be surprised to learn that Sterne does not deal with the concept of time in the same way as a realist writer. To begin with, let us try to clarify the difference.

**What are the obvious differences between the realist treatment of time and Sterne's in *Tristram Shandy*?**

## DISCUSSION

Here is my list of the differences:

| *Time in a Realist Novel* | *Time in Tristram Shandy* |
|---|---|
| 1 Time and its management is usually a hidden aspect of a realist novel. | Time and its management is foregrounded as one of the main themes of *Tristram Shandy*. |
| 2 Narrator assumes a consensus with the reader about chronological time. | Narrator makes a distinction between chronological and subjective time, and draws the reader's attention to the difference. |
| 3 Events and 'technical' aspects of the novel (e.g. the preface) are usually in chronological order. Cause precedes effect. | Preface is inserted in the middle of the novel. Events are not in chronological order. Effects often precede cause. |
| 4 Narrator does not mention the time it's taking to write the book. | Narrator continually mentions the time it's taking him to write *Tristram Shandy*. |
| 5 Narrator does not usually mention the time it takes for someone to read the book. | Narrator talks to an imaginary reader about the time it takes to read parts of *Tristram Shandy*. |
| 6 The action of the novel progresses. | The action of the novel regresses. |

Your list may well be different, but I think it would be reasonable to assume that in your 'Realist' column the concept of time is far less prominent than it is in *Tristram Shandy*. In a realist novel there are of course rigorous conventions brought into operation with regard to time, but our attention is not drawn to them. As I mentioned in Chapter 2, what a conventional novelist does, discreetly, is to skip years or months with phrases such as 'some years later' or 'in due course'. A novel may cover scores or hundreds of years and take us only hours to read. This discrepancy is so taken for granted that we seldom think about it. Realist novels also give us the psychological satisfaction of a completion or an ending, which we seldom have with such neatness in real life. In a famous formulation,

Henry James sums up one of the essential differences between reality and fiction:

> Really, universally, relations stop nowhere, and the exquisite problem of the artist is eternally but to draw, by a geometry of his own, the circle within which they happily *appear* to do so. He is in the perpetual predicament that the continuity of things is the whole matter, for him, of comedy and tragedy; that this continuity is never, by the space of an instant or an inch, broken, and that, to do anything at all, he has at once intensely to consult and intensely to ignore it.[1]

For a realist writer, the consulting has to be done in secret, without involving the reader. Sterne, however, is openly puzzled about the author's predicament. When in a character's life should the novel start? At what point do you end if the character is still alive? He is fascinated with the 'exquisite problem of the artist', but it is not a fascination he engages with silently: he shares it with the reader, step by step.

One of the fundamental problems of *Tristram Shandy*, both for Sterne and the reader, is that of chronology. 'Chronology' means the arrangement of events in order according to the times of their occurrence. The pattern of birth, life and death ensures for most of us an inbuilt understanding of chronology. This is reinforced by the wholly artificial but universally accepted system of naming and dividing 'time' into years, months, days, hours. Whatever spiritual or philosophical reservations we may have about these arrangements we tend to submit to them for the sake of convenience. A realist writer utilizes these conventions and operates in a chronological mode. Some flashbacks or background information may be given in order that the reader is sufficiently informed about the characters, but after that the action is usually given in a linear sequence. The terminology of novel criticism—beginning, middle, end, development, flashback—is inevitably linked with the notion of causality. Sterne's great contemporaries, Fielding and Richardson, made suspense (what will happen next?) a central component of their novels. We turn the pages to find out whether Tom Jones or Clarissa Harlow will survive the vicissitudes they undergo. Clearly, *Tristram Shandy* differs from these novels in that its events do not proceed in chronological order, and the element of suspense becomes so attenuated as to be negligible. This is not to say that the narrative of *Tristram Shandy* does not have a precise and stable framework of events and their dates, and some industrious critics have reconstructed a coherent linear sequence of actions.[2] But Sterne does not present them in chronological order, he does not offer cause and then effect to enable the narrative to achieve a linear progression. When Sterne dates an event he simply identifies it in time, but he does not give it a causal relationship with the next event he describes. Thus future and past do not refer to chronological time, but simply to the order of events in the narration. While talking about Tristram's birth in 1718, Sterne can promise to tell us of Uncle Toby's love affairs later in the novel, which in fact took place in 1713.

Sterne is only too aware of the difficulties of presenting an orderly narrative, and he shares his anxieties with the reader:

> I must give you some account of an adventure of Trim's, though much against my will. I say much against my will, only because the story, in one sense, is certainly out of its place here; for by right it should come in, either amongst the anecdotes of my uncle Toby's amours with widow Wadman, in which Corporal Trim was no mean actor,—or else in the middle of his and my uncle Toby's campaigns on the bowling-green,—for it will do very well in either place;—but then if I reserve it for either of those parts of my story,—I ruin the story I'm upon,—and if I tell it here—I anticipate matters, and ruin it there. (III, 23, p. 215)

No novelist is exempt from such technical problems, but they are seldom shared with the reader. Realizing the enormity of his task, Sterne appeals in desperation to a higher authority:

> O ye POWERS! (for powers ye are, and great ones too)—which enable mortal man to tell a story worth the hearing,——that kindly shew him, where he is to begin it,—and where he is to end it,—what he is to put into it,—and what he is to leave out,— (III, 23, p. 215)

A similar worry besets him a few chapters later:

> My mother, you must know——but I have fifty things more necessary to let you know first,—I have a hundred difficulties which I have promised to clear up, and a thousand distresses and domestic misadventures crowding in upon me thick and threefold, one upon the neck of another,—— (III, 38, p. 240)

He does not submit to the pressure of chronology, however, but defies it in both obvious and subtle ways. For example, in the middle of Volume III he stops to write 'The Author's Preface', since 'All my heroes are off my hands;—'tis the first time I have had a moment to spare,—' (III, 20, p. 202). In Volume IX he omits Chapters 18 and 19, leaving instead blank pages for them, but then inserts them after Chapter 25 'that it may be a lesson to the world, *to let people tell their stories their own way*' (IX, 25). These are perhaps obvious games with chronology, a deliberate flouting of the conventions which Sterne sees as inadequate for conveying the quality of Tristram's consciousness.

# Time

The following examples are more complicated. Would you read them, and consider what Sterne is doing with chronology in each case.

1. ——a cow broke in (to-morrow morning) to my uncle Toby's fortifications, and eat up two ratios and half of dried grass, tearing up the sods with it . . .   (III, 38, p. 240)
2. —Now this is the most puzzled skein of all—for in this last chapter, as far at least as it has helped me through Auxerre, I have been getting forwards in two different journeys together, and with the same dash of the pen—for I have got entirely out of Auxerre in this journey which I am writing now, and I am got half way out of Auxerre in that which I shall write hereafter—There is but a certain degree of perfection in everything; and by pushing at something beyond that, I have brought myself into such a situation, as no traveller ever stood before me; for I am at this moment walking across the market-place of Auxerre with my father and my uncle Toby, in our way back to dinner—and I am this moment also entering Lyons with my post-chaise broke into a thousand pieces—and I am moreover this moment in a handsome pavilion built by Pringello, upon the banks of the Garonne . . .   (VII, 28, p. 492)
3. Time wastes too fast: every letter I trace tells me with what rapidity Life follows my pen; the days and hours of it, more precious, my dear Jenny! than the rubies about thy neck, are flying over our heads like light clouds of a windy day, never to return more—every thing presses on—whilst thou art twisting that lock,—see! it grows grey;   (IX, 8, p. 582)

## DISCUSSION

In these extracts it seems to me that Sterne plays three different tricks on sequential narrative. In the first one he muddles the past tense with future time, so that the reader is given a preview of events which the narrator has not yet told. This reminds us that a story is predetermined, and that the author/narrator is always one step ahead of the reader, however much Sterne seeks to persuade us of his utter spontaneity. In the second extract the process is more complicated. Tristram as narrator superimposes two journeys upon each other, so that the narration covers both his trip to France as a young man with his father and Uncle Toby, and his return journey in adulthood. And he is also aware of the present, when he is in Toulouse, writing about the two earlier journeys. The consciousness encompasses both past and present simultaneously, and in this passage Sterne is trying to express that complexity. Memories are not simply a looking back, but can be a flooding of the present, and it is this convergence Sterne is attempting to force words towards. It is possible to imagine him attempting to do this typographically, by over-printing the account of his present journey on the account of his past journey. But perhaps the technical problems of this deterred even Sterne!

In the third extract his treatment of time becomes almost surreal. In order to convey his sense of time passing swiftly, he conflates present and future and imagines Jenny's hair growing grey as he watches, like a speeded-up film. This macabre image is very effective, and rather unnerving. Sterne's own treatment of time in this novel is so subjective that the reader's sense of everyday chronology can be severely shaken.

It gradually becomes clear from the accumulation of such examples that conventional chronology, in Sterne's view, is a falsification of experience, and in *Tristram Shandy* he explores two ideas of time. First, he conveys his awareness that the segmentation of time into years, months and days is an artificial device, and also undermines any assumptions that the perception of time falls neatly into categories of past, present and future. Secondly, he looks at the way in which time becomes subjective according to each person's experience, and he makes a distinction between clock time and psychological time.

The first idea, that of collapsing the distinction between past, present and future, has been made familiar to us by such thinkers as Freud and Einstein, as well as from our own experiences. Certain sensory perceptions, particularly those of taste and smell, can re-create in us the sensations we experienced long ago. (Proust's 'madeleine' is perhaps the most famous literary example of this experience, and it is to Modernist writers we look to find a nonlinear treatment of time in the novel.) What is important about such moments is that we do not merely 'remember' or 'predict' from a distinctive present: there is, as it were, a *fusion* of past and present. More common than these occurrences is the way in which our minds dart backwards and forwards in time, re-creating the past, or recalling it, and anticipating the future. In reality, no day can be experienced as a simple progression from morning to evening. We do not think in simple chronology, nor is our experience of living chronological except in the simplest biological terms. When Sterne writes simultaneously about his childhood and adult visits to France, he is trying to capture the ways in which past and present converge, and he is also aware of the difficulties involved in expressing such an experience in linear form. To try to overcome these limitations, *Tristram Shandy* is made up of discrete scenes which have a sense of timelessness in that they are all presented to us through Tristram's consciousness. He remembers, anticipates and undergoes present experience, and the shape of the narration is the sprawling, unordered configuration of both his unconscious and conscious minds. In trying to express the aims of Modernism, Virginia Woolf wrote:

> Let us record the atoms as they fall upon the mind in the order in which they fall, let us trace the pattern, however disconnected and incoherent in appearance, which each sight or incident scores upon the consciousness.[3]

This could be used as a very accurate description of the narrative method of *Tristram Shandy*.

Sterne's second idea of time is to make a distinction between chronological and psychological time. This distinction is of course familiar to us from personal experience: an hour spent at a boring lecture can seem an eternity; an hour with a lover may seem to last only a few minutes or can seem timeless. Sometimes the hands of the clock seem almost to stand still; at other times they seem to move faster than usual. Sterne's view of subjective time was influenced by John Locke, who put forward a theory of time based on what he called 'duration':

> ... It is evident to anyone who will but observe what passes in his own mind, that there is a train of ideas which constantly succeed one another in his understanding as long as he is awake. Reflection on these appearances of several ideas one after another in our minds, is that which furnishes us with the idea of succession; and the distance between any parts of that succession, or between the appearance of any two ideas in our minds, is what we call duration.[4]

In other words, Locke suggests that 'duration'—length of time—is experienced as the space between thoughts (the word 'distance' seems to conflate both 'time' and 'space'). This links in with the well-known assertion that if you are mentally active time passes quickly. In *Tristram Shandy* Walter talks about subjective time and clock time:

> It is two hours, and ten minutes,—and no more,—cried my father, looking at his watch, since Dr Slop and Obadiah arrived,—and I know not how it happens, brother Toby,—but to my imagination it seems almost an age.    (III, 18, pp. 198–9)

He then goes on to explain to a puzzled Toby, Locke's theory of time, at some length, and complains that clock time is endangering our awareness of psychological time:

> ... in our computation of *time*, we are so used to minutes, hours, weeks, and months,—and of clocks (I wish there was not a clock in the kingdom) to measure out their several portions to us, and to those who belong to us,—that 'twill be well, if in time to come, *the*

*succession of our ideas* be of any use or service to us at all. (III, 18, p. 200)

In *Time in Literature* Hans Meyerhoff describes the mixture of dimensions which makes up the narrative process of a work of biography or literature:

> The literary reconstruction of one's life invariably involves two dimensions: a subjective pattern of significant associations (poetry) and an objective structure of verifiable biographical and historical events (truth). Both dimensions are present, not only in biographical and autobiographical forms of literature, but in any literary portrait whatsoever. There is no way of constructing a man's life, whether real or fictional, except through reconstructing his past in terms of significant associations supervening upon the objective, historical data, or except through showing the inseparable intermixture of the two dimensions. What may be called a 'literary reconstruction' of man has always used, in addition to the objective, historical data, the pattern of significant associations in the stream of consciousness and in memory as the most important clue to the structure of the personality or the identity of the self.[5]

*Tristram Shandy*, a fictional autobiography, has its own 'historical data', but these are subordinated throughout to a 'subjective pattern of significant associations'. If you represent the (admittedly sparse) events of Tristram Shandy's life as a horizontal line, the 'significant associations' could be shown as vertical lines representing the digressions moving to and from the central narrative. The resulting diagram would, I suggest, have so many vertical lines that it would be easy to see why the novel does not progress very far.

Sterne was also very interested in the relationship between time as portrayed in a novel, and real, chronological time. Would you now reread the extraordinary chapter where he discusses this relationship in Volume II, Chapter 8. What is Sterne's argument about time in this chapter?

## DISCUSSION

Sterne begins this chapter with a reflexive reference to an event he has described three pages before:

> It is about an hour and a half's tolerable good reading since my uncle Toby rung the bell, when Obadiah was ordered to saddle a horse, and go for Dr Slop, the man-midwife;—so that no one can say, with reason, that I have not allowed Obadiah time enough, poetically speaking, and considering the emergency too, both to go and come;
> —— (p. 122)

This 'hour and a half's good reading' refers to the fact that Uncle Toby's act of ringing the bell is interrupted by the narrator in Volume I, Chapter 21, who begins a long digression. The narrator estimates that this first digression (which finishes in Volume II, Chapter 6) will take the reader an hour and a half to read. Here he is trying to pretend a correlation between the time an action would take in reality, and the time it takes to read about it. But as the action is taken up again only three pages before Sterne's reference to it, with Obadiah being sent to summon Dr Slop, the narrator has to admit that in real time the reader has probably taken only about two minutes to read the second digression. But he then argues that we are not dealing with real time, but with psychological time and the idea of duration as defined by Locke. The narrator points out that although it may have taken us only two minutes or so to read the intervening material, it covered a time span of four years, and the distance from Flanders to England. And, he concludes in triumph, it is surely therefore a long enough 'duration' for the reader to imagine Obadiah's having sufficient time for his journey of eight miles and back to fetch Dr Slop. In other words, Sterne is here acknowledging both the 'clock-time' ('two minutes, thirteen seconds and three-fifths'—one wonders if he timed it) it takes to read the three pages of the novel, and the 'novel-time' (four years compressed into the same duration). In the last paragraph he imagines a 'hypercritic' adhering rigidly to the 'two minutes, thirteen seconds' of reading time, whom he imagines to be still complaining that this isn't sufficient time for Obadiah to travel sixteen miles. In order to 'put an end to the whole objection and controversy' Sterne suddenly and audaciously changes his story by saying that Obadiah did not in fact have to travel that distance after all, as he 'had not got above three-score yards from the stable-yard before he met with Dr Slop'. So, it is implied, the meeting could have been achieved within two minutes, thirteen seconds, thus satisfying the imaginary 'hypercritic' who demands that the events of the novel take exactly the same time as the telling of them. The sophistication of this chapter is considerable, and its humour depends on our awareness of Sterne's comic exploitation of four time schemes: the real clock time it takes us to read a few pages of a novel; the real clock time it would take Obadiah to ride sixteen miles on horseback in winter, the compression of time in a novel where four years may be spanned in a few seconds, and the psychological experience of duration in a novel where a few pages can take only a few minutes to read, yet enable us to believe that several years have passed. This chapter is one of the most dazzling in the whole novel, and Sterne displays a certain amount of courage in that, having destroyed the reader's conviction of the veracity of 'novel-time' (the temporal world he or she needs to be convinced of whilst reading a novel), he expects us to go on reading it, however disorientating the experience might be.

Sterne frequently makes comments about the length of time it takes either to write or to read a passage of *Tristram Shandy*. For example: 'Stay—I have a small account to settle with the reader before Trim can go on with his harangue.—It shall be done in two minutes' (V, 8, p. 357). Or, when referring to the incident of the hot chestnut: 'Though this has taken up some time in the narrative, it took up little more time in the transaction' (IV, 27, p. 319). His main worry, however, surfaces early in the novel, and recurs throughout it.

**Would you now reread Volume I, Chapter 14; Volume IV, Chapter 13; and Volume V, Chapter 16. What is the theme linking these chapters, and what is the source of their humour?**

## DISCUSSION

The theme linking all three chapters is the problem of infinite regression. As early as Volume I of his *Life and Opinions* the narrator, Tristram, begins to be anxious about the amount of material he feels it necessary to include in his book:

> To sum up all; there are archives at every stage to be looked into, and rolls, records, documents, and endless genealogies, which justice ever and anon calls him back to stay the reading of:—In short, there is no end of it;—for my own part, I declare I have been at it these six weeks, making all the speed I possibly could,—and am not yet born:—I have just been able, and that's all, to tell you *when* it happened, but not *how*;—so that you see the thing is yet far from being accomplished. (I, 14, p. 65)

This problem of regression begins to obsess the narrator, and his attention to it questions the viability of realism, which strives to give the impression of effortless all-inclusion. Sterne refuses to give that impression, and draws attention to the fact that something has to be left out if the book is to be finished—or even if the narrator is to be born. At the beginning of this chapter Sterne vigorously defends digression as the mark of a 'man of spirit', yet, for all that, he realizes that digressions will run counter to the progress of the novel.

In Volume IV the same theme is pursued, except that the difficulty is now more acute:

> I am this month one whole year older than I was this time twelvemonth; and having got, as you perceive, almost into the middle of my fourth volume—and no farther than to my first day's life—'tis demonstrative that I have three hundred and sixty-four days more life

> to write just now, than when I first set out; so that instead of advancing, as a common writer, in my work with what I have been doing at it—on the contrary, I am just thrown so many volumes back—was every day of my life to be as busy a day as this—And why not?—and the transactions and opinions of it to take up as much description—And for what reason should they be cut short? as at this rate I should just live 364 times faster than I should write—It must follow, an' please your worships, that the more I write, the more I shall have to write—and consequently, the more your worships read, the more your worships will have to read.   (IV, 13, p. 286)

The narrator can never catch up with the proliferation of past events, and so is overtaken by them. As we have seen, he believes that an account of his birth entails, at the very least, a description of his conception, the details of his mother's marriage settlement, and a history of the local midwife and male-midwife, not to mention all the other incidental digressions embarked on by his father and Uncle Toby. What is so comic about this passage is the rising note of panic in it, and the narrator's desperation when he realizes that there is no reason why every day should not be as busy as the day on which he's writing, and its events take just as long to describe. Henry James says of literary selection that it

> is really a business to terrify all but stout hearts into abject omission and mutilation, though the terror would indeed be more general were the general consciousness of the difficulty greater.[6]

Sterne, through his narrator, is acutely conscious of the difficulty, and the absurd paradox is that the more he talks about it, the worse he makes it.

The apparent impossibility of the narrator's task is comically paralleled by Walter Shandy's attempts at authorship. Realizing that Tristram's conception, nose and name have all been cut short through unfortunate accidents (this is before the final unfortunate accident with the sash window), Walter decides to try to remedy these deficiencies by writing an encyclopaedia on child-rearing specifically for the education of his son; a 'Tristra-paedia'. But unfortunately for Walter he suffers the same difficulties as Tristram and John de la Casse, an archbishop invented and quoted by the narrator who managed to write only a line and a half a day. The terrible and comic irony of Walter's undertaking is that Tristram outgrows the manual before it is written:

> the misfortune was, that I was all that time totally neglected and abandoned to my mother; and what was almost as bad, by the very delay, the first part of the work, upon which my father had spent the most of his pains, was rendered entirely useless,—every day a page or two became of no consequence.—   (V, 16, pp. 368–9)

The humour of these passages lies in the contrast between what we know of a realist writer's ruthless treatment of time, and Tristram's increasing scruples about it. His anxiety about what is usually taken for granted is comic. It is also comically irrelevant because, as James Swearingen points out:

> How can he possibly be serious in saying that we shall have an hour of reading for each hour of living when he makes no effort . . . to give us anything of the actual texture of his daily life?[7]

Tristram's material (except in Volume VII, which we'll look at later) is so random, his time schemes so various, that a day-to-day account of living would be an aberration in the context of *Tristram Shandy*.

As we've discovered, the distinction between 'narrator' and Sterne is shifting and uncertain. In the treatment of 'time' is it the views of the narrator, or of the novelist that we are grappling with?

**Would you now reread this paragraph in Volume IV, Chapter 13, in which Tristram says of his increasingly long book:**

> Will this be good for your worships' eyes?
> It will do well for mine; and, was it not that my OPINIONS will be the death of me, I perceive I shall lead a fine life of it out of this self-same life of mine; or, in other words, shall lead a couple of fine lives together.
> As for the proposal of twelve volumes a year, or a volume a month, it no way alters my prospect—write as I will, and rush as I may into the middle of things, as Horace advises,—I shall never overtake myself——whipped and driven to the last pinch, at the worst I shall have one day the start of my pen—and one day is enough for two volumes—and two volumes will be enough for one year.    (IV, 13, p. 286)

Does this seem problematic to you, and if so, why?

## DISCUSSION

In this paragraph, as in many others throughout the novel, I am confused about the 'I' figure. Is it Tristram, or is it Sterne? This distinction between author and narrator is accentuated when Sterne/Tristram talks about time. It seems to me that here Sterne himself is talking about the enterprise of writing a novel entitled *The Life and Opinions of Tristram Shandy, Gentleman*. The 'couple of fine lives together' refer to those of Sterne and Tristram, and the mention of death reminds us that Sterne suffers increasingly from consumption during the writing of this book. When Sterne/Tristram says 'I shall never overtake myself' he seems to be saying that the novel *is* in some way a real account of his life. It is Sterne's autobiographical fiction, presented as Tristram Shandy's autobiography.

There are other instances where the author appears to step very directly into the narration and change its tone.
**Consider the following examples:**

1. '... it is no more than a week from this very day, in which I am now writing this book for the edification of the world,—which is March 9, 1759,—that my dear, dear Jenny ... stood cheapening a silk of five-and-twenty shillings a yard ...'   (I, 18, p. 72)
2. '... that observation is my own;—and was struck out by me this very rainy day, March 26, 1759, and betwixt the hours of nine and ten in the morning.'   (I, 21)
3. 'And here I am sitting, this 12th day of August, 1766, in a purple jerkin and a yellow pair of slippers, without either wig or cap on ...'   (IX, 1, p. 572)

**Do they strike you as different from the dominant narrative tone of _Tristram Shandy_? If so, what constitutes the difference?**

DISCUSSION

These passages seem to me to be highly personal, an intervention into the narrative where Sterne the author overpowers, as it were, Tristram the narrator. Phrases such as 'this very day', 'I am now writing', 'this very rainy day', 'betwixt nine and ten', 'this 12th day of August, 1766' make me feel absolutely convinced that Laurence Sterne was actually writing those words on the days he describes. Certainly they occur in the appropriate volumes—that is, the dates are consistent with the serial publication of the novel. So, throughout _Tristram Shandy_, in addition to the narrator's games with time, there is an historical time scheme based on Sterne's real life: his writing schedule, his health, his travels. This sometimes intrudes on Tristram's fictional time scheme, which is concerned with his birth and upbringing, and with characters such as Yorick, Walter Shandy and Toby. The authorial interventions are sometimes difficult to separate from the narrator's direct comments to the reader, but they seem particularly distinctive when referring to the passing of time, or the precise marking of it: 'this very day'.

Time as a theme dominates Volume VII, where the immediate and heightened narration takes a different form from specific authorial intervention. This volume begins:

> No—I think, I said, I would write two volumes every year, provided the vile cough which then tormented me, and which to this hour I

dread worse than the devil, would but give me leave... (VII, 1, p. 459)

It is the 'vile cough' which in reality took Sterne to the South of France to a warmer climate, and this volume is concerned with Tristram's flight from Death, which is personified as a pursuing figure from whom Tristram is escaping. It is the most chronologically straightforward of the volumes of *Tristram Shandy*; at first there are very few digressions, as if Death were truly on the heels of the narrator and he needs to move quickly—but later, as Tristram reaches the South of France and his health improves, the style becomes more discursive once again. This sense of urgency, of time passing, is vividly captured in Chapter 9, in the narrator's description of the inn-keeper's daughter, Janatone:

> But he who measures thee, Janatone, must do it now—thou carriest the principles of change within thy frame; and considering the chances of a transitory life, I would not answer for thee a moment. (VII, 9, p. 469)

Awareness of mortality permeates Volume VII, and as William V. Holtz points out, it is paradoxically

> the only real digression in *Tristram Shandy*. The other books all have their roots in the unity of Tristram's mind and his attempts to reveal it, but the seventh book takes its impetus from an event in a sense external to his material—the overt threat of death's intrusion into the hermetic world of imaginative recall.[8]

It seems a less rich volume than the others, and I think this is because we have become so used to Sterne's games with time, his deliberate and ingenious refusals to submit to the conventional demands of chronology, that a linear narrative seems thin in comparison. The experience of a narrative governed by time, instead of exploiting it, comes as a surprise at this stage of *Tristram Shandy*, and it's with some relief that we realize that in Volume VIII Sterne is well enough, as it were, to return to his familiar, digressive style.

\* \* \*

When Sterne began to write the first volume of *Tristram Shandy* he was forty-six years old, unhappily married, undistinguished, impecunious, and suffering from consumption. Life had not been good to him, and it is not difficult to imagine his writing *Tristram Shandy* as a final attempt to make his mark, to put on record, as it were, his extraordinary personality for all time. Throughout the seven years of the novel's publication, Sterne is aware of the possibility of his imminent death, and this awareness helps to explain his obsession with time and chronology within the novel. Sometimes his attitude to them is playful, sometimes defiant, but always he tries to outwit, through recollection and imagination, a sense of time's passing. Time as a persistent underlying theme in *Tristram Shandy* suggests Sterne's acute anxiety about it, which is successfully disguised until it bursts out in Volume VII. The passage of real time brings death, and throughout the novel we can see a correlation with its ending and the end of life. Both Sterne and Tristram struggle against the inevitability of chronology, and this real tension gives *Tristram Shandy* a sense of urgency and immediacy. Sterne's instantly intimate style, his confiding tone, can be seen as the voice of someone who cannot waste time with distance and formality. His 'vile cough' acts as a perpetual *memento mori*, and this is both his motivation and, obliquely, his theme. *Tristram Shandy* could be subtitled *Sterne versus Time*, and of course Sterne knew that in one sense time would beat him in the end. Both he and *The Life and Opinions of Tristram Shandy* eventually have to finish, but he does not give up without a struggle. 'I must take up again the pen', he writes in May 1766. 'In faith I think I shall die with it in my hand'.[9] There is a critical debate about whether Sterne actually completed *Tristram Shandy*, or merely ceased writing it.[10] On 30 August, 1766 he wrote, 'I shall publish the 9th & 10 of Shandy the next winter',[11] but he became increasingly ill and tired, and never wrote the tenth volume. *Tristram Shandy* seems to me to be left with the potential for further volumes, but its sense of incompletion is very appropriate to a novel which runs against the clock, and ends, in chronological terms, before the time of its beginning.

Sterne was well aware of the power of words over time past, and makes this clear in Volume VIII, in a conversation between Corporal Trim and Uncle Toby, about Trim's story of the king of Bohemia:

> —'Tis thy own, Trim, so ornament it after thy own fashion; and take any date, continued my uncle Toby, looking pleasantly upon him—take any date in the whole world thou choosest, and put it to—thou art heartily welcome—
> The corporal bowed; for of every century, and of every year of that century, from the first creation of the world down to Noah's flood; and from Noah's flood to the birth of Abraham; through all the pilgrimages of the patriarchs, to the departure of the Israelites out of Egypt——and throughout all the Dynasties, Olympiads, Urbeconditas, and other memorable epochs of the different nations of the world, down to the coming of Christ, and from thence to the very moment in which the corporal was telling his story—had my uncle Toby subjected this vast empire of time and its abysses at his feet.  (VIII, 19, p. 536)

But Sterne goes further in his battle with time in *Tristram Shandy*. His purpose is not merely to defeat time but, like Proust, to redeem time through the transcendence of art. In this he succeeds triumphantly. Volume by volume he ensures his timelessness, and in the final reckoning he does outwit chronology. His work lives on after his death, and it lives on with an enormous, overflowing vitality. Sterne's irrepressible zest for life (sharpened, maybe, by the implications of his 'vile cough') comes over two hundred years later with clarity and exuberance. For all its sniping at critics and clerics, its inadequate accounts of women, what shines out from *Tristram Shandy* is Sterne's intense fascination with his fellow human beings, and his faith in the potential goodness of human kind.

\* \* \*

To end this *Guide*, I should like to offer you two quotations about time and the artistic process.

1. The man is a human being of normal appetites and desires, for whom life is essentially the process of dying. The artist is a free, detached spirit which looks down on the man from a distance and is concerned not so much with the consumption of life as with the transcendence of life through creative effort. The man must spend himself, but the artist-spirit saves itself by becoming one with its works and thus escaping the bonds of time . . . To escape death and become immortal, the artist-self would somehow remove himself from the bonds of chronological time which drives him relentlessly from cradle to grave. Opposed to chronological time is subjective time, which cannot be clocked: minutes are sometimes hours, hours can be minutes. But for most of us, such time is as fleeting, as transitory, as the seconds the clock ticks off. What the artist tries to do is to capture lost time and imprison it in the form of his art-work. The man must die, but the artist in him can achieve immortality in his works.[12]
2. . . . the cruel law of art is that people die and we ourselves die after exhausting every form of suffering, so that over our heads may grow the grass not of oblivion but of eternal life, the vigorous and luxuriant growth of a true work of art, and so that thither, gaily and without a thought for those who are sleeping beneath them, future generations may enjoy their *déjeuner sur l'herbe*.[13]

After you have read these extracts, please go on thinking about them, their relevance to each other, and to the theme of time in *Tristram Shandy*.

# Notes

**Chapter 1—Introduction (pages 1–9)**

1. David Thomson, *Wild Excursions: The Life and Fiction of Laurence Sterne* (Weidenfeld and Nicholson, 1972), p. 22.
2. Coleridge, *Biographia Literaria*, ch. 14 (Everyman's Library, 1956), p. 169.

**Chapter 2—Contextual (pages 9–22)**

1. *Memoirs of the Life and Family of the late Rev. Mr Laurence Sterne*. First published by Lydia de Medalle (Sterne's daughter) in *Letters of the late Rev. Mr Laurence Sterne* (London, 1775). Included in L. P. Curtis, *Letters of Laurence Sterne* (Clarendon Press, 1935), p. 2.
2. See Arthur H. Cash, *Laurence Sterne: The Early and Middle Years* (Methuen, 1975), p. 20.
3. Sterne, *Memoirs*, op. cit., pp. 3–4.
4. Laurence Sterne, Letter to Archdeacon Sterne, 5 April 1751, in Curtis, *op. cit.*, p. 34.
5. Quoted by David Thomson, *op. cit.*, p. 99. From Emily J. Climenson, *Elizabeth Montagu, The Queen of the Blue-Stockings, Her Correspondence 1720–1761* (London, 1906), Vol. I, p. 73.
6. Quoted by Arthur H. Cash, *op. cit.*, p. 84.
7. Sterne, *Memoirs*, op. cit., p. 5.
8. Sterne, Letter to David Garrick, 27 January 1760. From Curtis, *op. cit.*, p. 77.
9. See Max Byrd, *Tristram Shandy* (George Allen and Unwin, 1985), p. 24, where he points out that Sterne wittily criticizes plagiarism by himself plagiarizing Robert Burton.
10. See Wayne Booth, 'The Self-Conscious Narrator in Comic Fiction before *Tristram Shandy*', *PMLA* (March 1952), pp. 162–85.
11. See D. W. Jefferson, '*Tristram Shandy* and the Tradition of Learned Wit', *Essays in Criticism*, I (1951). Reprinted in *Laurence Sterne: A Collection of Critical Essays*, John Traugott (ed.) (Prentice Hall, 1968), pp. 148–67.
12. John Locke, *Essay Concerning Human Understanding*, Book II, ch. 1, Section 2. John W. Yolton (ed.) Everyman's Library (Dent, 1961).
13. *Ibid.* Book II, chapter 33, section 5.
14. Ian Watt, *The Rise of the Novel: Studies in Defoe, Richardson and Fielding* (Chatto and Windus, 1957; Peregrine Books, 1963), p. 33.

15 A fascinating book which examines the historical and cultural influences on the evolution of realism is Erich Auerbach's *Mimesis* (Princeton University Press, 1953).

## Chapter 3—Sentiment, Sexuality and the Reader's Role (pages 22–41)

1 Correspondence of Samuel Richardson, 1804, IV, pp. 282–3. Quoted by Henri Fluchère, *Laurence Sterne: From Tristram to Yorick: An Interpretation of Tristram Shandy*, trans. by Barbara Bray, (O.U.P., 1965) p. 370.
2 See John Traugott's interesting discussion of the word 'sentimentalism' in his introduction to *Laurence Sterne: A Collection of Critical Essays*, p. 4.
3 William Hazlitt, *Lectures on the English Comic Writers*, quoted in *Sterne: The Critical Heritage*, Alan B. Howes (ed.) (Routledge and Kegan Paul, 1974) p. 361.
4 William Makepeace Thackeray, *The English Humorists*, M. R. Ridley (ed.) (Dent, 1968), pp. 233–4.
5 Wordsworth, Preface to *Lyrical Ballads* (1802) in *Wordsworth's Literary Criticism*, W. J. B. Owen (ed.) (Routledge and Kegan Paul, 1974), p. 85.
6 For a further discussion of the 'Comedy of Displacement' see A. R. Towers, 'Sterne's Cock and Bull Story', *ELH*, Vol. 24, No. 1, March 1957, pp. 12–29.
7 See, in particular, Wolfgang Iser, *The Implied Reader: Patterns of Communication in Prose Fiction from Bunyan to Beckett* (The Johns Hopkins University Press, 1974), and Jane P. Tompkins, *Reader–Response Criticism* (Baltimore, 1980).
8 *Sterne: The Critical Heritage*, Alan B. Howes (ed.) p. 70.
9 Ian Watt, (ed.) Introduction to *Tristram Shandy* (Cambridge, 1984), p. xliv.

## Chapter 4—Characterization (pages 41–59)

1 Henry Fielding, *Tom Jones*, Vol. I, ch. 2 (1789)
2 George Eliot, *Middlemarch*, Bk. I, ch. 12 (1871)
3 Laurence Sterne, *Tristram Shandy*, Vol. I, ch. 21 (1760)
4 In a letter about an earlier novel George Eliot wrote to her publisher: 'My artistic bent is not at all to the presentation of eminently irreproachable characters, but to the presentation of mixed human beings in such a way as to call forth tolerant judgment, pity and sympathy. And I cannot stir a step aside from what I *feel* to be *true* in character'. Letter to John Blackwood, 1857. Quoted by Gordon S. Haight in *George Eliot: A Biography* (The Clarendon Press, 1968), p. 222.
5 Sterne, letter (recipient unknown) 30 January 1760. L. P. Curtis, *op. cit.*, p. 88.
6 John Locke, *An Essay Concerning Human Understanding*, *op. cit.*, Book III, chapter II, section 1.
7 'You would be apt to paint Trim . . .' (p. 138)
'. . . to take the picture of him . . .' (p. 138)
'. . . the limits of the line of beauty . . .' (p. 138)

'... this I recommend to painters ...' (p. 139)
'a statuary might have modelled from it.' (p. 139)
8. Sterne, letter to Richard Berenger, ?8 March 1760. L. P. Curtis, p. 101. In *The Analysis of Beauty* Hogarth talks about the eloquence of action and how economically it can be conveyed in art: 'action is a sort of language ... The general idea of an action, as well as of an attitude, may be given with a pencil in a very few lines'. *The Analysis of Beauty*, Richard Woodfield (ed.) (reprinted by Scolar Press, Menston 1971) p. 139.
9. Samuel Beckett, *Watt* (Calder and Boyars, 1963), p. 6.
10. Henri Fluchère, *op. cit.*, p. 339.
11. Sterne, letter to David Garrick, 27 January 1760. L. P. Curtis, p. 87.
12. For example, in a letter to Mrs F. written ?April 1765, and to Mrs Daniel Draper, written in March 1767. L. P. Curtis, pp. 241 and 319.
13. L. P. Curtis, p. 76.
14. Sterne, letter to David Garrick, 19 April 1762. L. P. Curtis, p. 163.
15. Sterne, letter to the Earl of ——, 28 November 1767. L. P. Curtis, pp. 402–3.
16. William Hazlitt, *Lectures on the English Comic Writers* in *Sterne: The Critical Heritage*, *op. cit.*, p. 361.
17. Alain Robbe-Grillet, 'A Future for the Novel' from *For a New Novel* in *Twentieth Century Literary Criticism: a Reader*, David Lodge (ed.) (Longman, 1972) p. 470.
18. Roland Barthes, *S/Z* (trans. Richard Miller) (Harvard University Press, 1974) p. 67.
19. Patricia Meyer Spacks, *Imagining a Self* (Harvard University Press, 1976) p. 11.
20. Lennard Davis, *Resisting Novels: Ideology and Fiction* (Methuen, 1987) p. 108.

## Chapter 5—Reflexive (pages 59–75)

1. William V. Holtz, *Image and Immortality: A Study of Tristram Shandy* (Brown University Press, 1970) p. 84.
2. William Hogarth, *The Analysis of Beauty*, *op. cit.*, p. 25.
3. *Ibid.*, pp. 38–9.
4. Terry Eagleton, *Literary Theory: An Introduction* (Blackwell, 1983) Preface.
5. Victor Shklovsky, 'Art as Technique' from *Russian Formalist Criticism: Four Essays*, Lemon and Reis (eds) (Lincoln, 1965) p. 12.
6. Victor Shklovsky, 'Sterne's *Tristram Shandy*: Stylistic Commentary', *Russian Formalist Criticism: Four Essays*, pp. 25–57.
7. *Ibid.*, pp. 30–1.

## Chapter 6—Time (pages 75–90)

1. Henry James, 'Preface to Roderick Hudson', from *The Art of the Novel*, (Charles Scribner's Sons, 1934), p. 5.
2. For example, Theodore Baird, 'The Time-Scheme of *Tristram Shandy* and a Source', *PMLA*, LI, September 1936, pp. 803–20, and Henri Fluchère: *Laurence Sterne: from Tristram to Yorick*, pp. 104–9.

3. Virginia Woolf, 'Modern Fiction' (from *The Common Reader I*) in *Collected Essays*, Vol. II (Hogarth Press, 1966), p. 107.
4. John Locke, *Essay Concerning Human Understanding*, op. cit. Book II, Chapter 14, Section 3.
5. Hans Meyerhoff, *Time in Literature* (Berkeley, 1955) pp. 64–84. Quoted by William V. Holtz in *Image and Immortality: a study of Tristram Shandy*, pp. 134–5.
6. Henry James, 'Preface to *Roderick Hudson*', op. cit. p. 14.
7. James Swearingen, *Reflexivity in Tristram Shandy: an essay in phenomenological criticism* (Yale University Press, 1977) p. 102.
8. William V. Holtz, op. cit., p. 133.
9. L. P. Curtis, p. 277.
10. See, for example, Wayne C. Booth, 'Did Sterne Complete *Tristram Shandy?*' *Modern Philology*, XLVII (February 1951) pp. 172–83; R. F. Brissenden, "Trusting to Almighty God": another look at the composition of *Tristram Shandy*', and Marcia Allentuck, 'In Defense of an Unfinished *Tristram Shandy*: Laurence Sterne and the *Non Finito*'. The last two articles are in *The Winged Skull: Essays on Laurence Sterne*, Cash and Stedmond (eds) (Methuen, 1971) pp. 259–69 and 145–55 respectively.
11. L. P. Curtis, p. 288.
12. Maurice Beebe, *Ivory Towers and Sacred Founts*, (New York, 1964), pp. 6–7, 11. Quoted by William V. Holtz, op. cit., p. 148.
13. Marcel Proust, 'Time Regained' in *Remembrance of Things Past*, trans. C. K. Scott Moncrieff and Terence Kilmartin; and by Andreas Mayor (Chatto and Windus, 1981; Penguin edition 1983) p. 1095.

# Suggestions for Further Reading

There are a great many books and articles published on Laurence Sterne. The following list is a short selection designed to guide you to the most useful of them.

**Other works by Sterne**

It is very helpful to read Sterne's other writings, which often shed light on aspects of *Tristram Shandy*. These are *A Political Romance*, *A Sentimental Journey* and *The Journal of Eliza*. They are published in one book edited by Ian Jack: *A Sentimental Journey Through France and Italy by Mr Yorick, To Which are Added The Journal to Eliza and A Political Romance* (Oxford University Press, 1968). A selection of Sterne's sermons is edited by Marjorie David, in *The Sermons of Mr Yorick* (Carcanet Press, 1973). Sterne's complete works are collected in twelve volumes by Wilbur L. Cross in his *Works and Life* (J. F. Taylor, 1904). Invaluable source material is to be found in *Letters of Laurence Sterne*, edited by L. P. Curtis (Oxford University Press, 1935). These letters are wonderful to read; their freshness and liveliness give great insight into Sterne's character.

**Bibliography**

A bibliography of Sterne criticism is to be found in Lodowick Hartley's books: *Laurence Sterne in the Twentieth Century: An Essay and a Bibliography of Sternean Studies, 1900–1965*, (University of North Carolina Press, 1966), and *Laurence Sterne: an annotated bibliography 1966–1977* (G. K. Hall, 1978). These are comprehensive and essential reading for anyone embarking on a study of Laurence Sterne's work. If you are interested in the history of the early editions of *Tristram Shandy*, see Kenneth Monkman's article 'The Bibliography of the Early Editions of *Tristram Shandy*', *The Library*, 5th series, vol. 25 (1970) pp. 11–39.

**Biography**

The standard biography of Sterne used to be Wilbur Cross's *The Life and Times of Laurence Sterne* (first published, 1909, revised edition Yale

University Press, 1925). This has now been supplemented by a more recent biography in two volumes, by Arthur H. Cash, *Laurence Sterne: the early and middle years* (Methuen, 1975) and *Laurence Sterne: the later years* (Methuen, 1986). This excellent biography also includes some critical commentary on Sterne's works, relating them to his life at the times of writing. A shorter biography, very perceptive and well-writen, is *Wild Excursions: the life and fiction of Laurence Sterne* by David Thomson (Weidenfeld and Nicolson, 1972).

### Critical

For a compendium of Sternean critical history, see the two books edited by Alan B. Howes: *Yorick and the Critics: Sterne's reputation in England 1760–1868* (Yale University Press, 1958) and *Sterne: The Critical Heritage* (Routledge and Kegan Paul, 1974). General books on Sterne include two collections of essays: *The Winged Skull: papers from the Laurence Sterne Bicentenary Conference at the University of York* (Methuen, 1971) edited by Arthur H. Cash and John M. Stedmond, and *Laurence Sterne: A Collection of Critical Essays* edited by John Trangott (Prentice-Hall, 1968). The latter collects together significant essays such as Victor Shklovsky's 'A Parodying Novel: Sterne's *Tristram Shandy*', and D. W. Jefferson's '*Tristram Shandy* and the Tradition of Learned Wit'. Perhaps the most thoroughgoing analysis of *Tristram Shandy* is *Laurence Sterne: From Tristram to Yorick: an interpretation of Tristram Shandy* by Henri Fluchère, translated by Barbara Bray (Oxford University Press, 1965). Fluchère begins with a chapter entitled 'How to Approach *Tristram Shandy*' and his book disentangles its themes clearly and in great detail. A good short book is Max Byrd's *Tristram Shandy* (George Allen and Unwin, 1985), which includes an excellent bibliography.

Some Sternean criticism links the written and pictorial arts, and useful background reading is Gotthold Lessing's *Laokoon* (1766) (translated by William A. Steel, Everyman's Library, Dent, 1930). This includes a discussion on the relationship between literature and painting, and together with William Hogarth's *The Analysis of Beauty* (1753) edited by Richard Woodfield (The Scolar Press, Menston 1971) is necessary reading for an advanced study of *Tristram Shandy*. A book which considers the relationship of the verbal and the visual in *Tristram Shandy* is *Image and Immortality: a study of Tristram Shandy* by William V. Holtz (Brown University Press, 1970). This is a very illuminating and important study. A book concerned with the structure (in its widest sense) of *Tristram Shandy* is *Laurence Sterne and the Argument About Design* by Mark Coveridge (Macmillan, 1982). This has a substantial bibliography.

As background to *Tristram Shandy* it is helpful to have read John Locke's *Essay Concerning Human Understanding* (1690), edited by John W. Yolton (Everyman's Library, Dent, 1961). John Traugott examines Sterne's use of Locke in *Tristram Shandy's World: Sterne's philosophical rhetoric* (University of California Press, 1954). Other philosophical studies include Helen Moglen's *The Philosophical Irony of Laurence Sterne* (University Presses of Florida, 1975), and *Reflexivity in Tristram Shandy: an essay in phenomenological criticism* (Yale University Press, 1977) by James E. Swearingen. Swearingen uses *Tristram Shandy* as a means of understanding the theories

# Suggestions for Further Reading 97

of Husserl and Heidegger, rather than *vice versa*, but this emphasis nevertheless illuminates *Tristram Shandy* also.

Books with chapters or substantial references to Sterne or *Tristram Shandy* include the following:

*The Rhetoric of Fiction* by Wayne C. Booth (University of Chicago Press, 1961) pp. 221–40. Booth examines the narrative method of *Tristram Shandy*.

*Resisting Novels* by Lennard J. Davis (Methuen, 1987) pp. 150–57. In his section on *Tristram Shandy* Davis looks at the relationship between narration and the creation of character.

*The Early Masters of English Fiction* by Alan Dugald Mckillop (University of Kansas Press, 1956) pp. 182–219. This chapter is reprinted in John Traugott's collection of essays, mentioned above.

*Time and the Novel* by A. A. Mendilow (Peter Nevill, 1952) pp. 158–99. This is also reprinted in Traugott, but the whole book is well worth reading as background to the concept of time in *Tristram Shandy*.

*The Created Self: The Reader's Role in Eighteenth Century Fiction* by John Preston (Heinemann, 1970) pp. 133–95. These chapters brilliantly analyse the ways in which Sterne uses and transposes the roles of author and reader in *Tristram Shandy*.

*Four Portraits: Studies of the Eighteenth Century* by Peter Quennell (Collins, 1945) pp. 139–94. A good, short biographical sketch of Sterne.

*Imagining a Self: Autobiography and Novel in Eighteenth Century England* by Patricia Meyer Spacks (Harvard University Press, 1976) pp. 127–57. This chapter looks at the relationship between Sterne, Tristram and the reader.

*The English Novel: Form and Function* by Dorothy van Ghent (Harper and Row, 1961, first published 1953) pp. 83–98. A very valuable chapter which looks at the structure of *Tristram Shandy* and compares Sterne with Modernist writers.

## Articles

The humour of Sterne is analysed by A. E. Dyson in 'Sterne: The Novelist as Jester' *The Critical Quarterly*, Vol. 4, No. 4, (Winter 1962) pp. 309–20, and also in D. W. Jefferson's '*Tristram Shandy* and the tradition of Learned Wit', *Essays in Criticism*, Vol. 1, (1951) pp. 225–48. This is also reprinted in Traugott's essay collection, pp. 148–67. 'Sterne's Cock and Bull Story' by A. R. Towers emphasizes the sexual element of Sterne's comedy *ELH*, Vol. 24 No. 1 (1957) pp. 12–29. The sexuality of *Tristram Shandy* is also discussed by Frank Brady in '*Tristram Shandy*: Sexuality, Morality and Sensibility' in *Eighteenth Century Studies*, Vol. 4, No. 1 (Fall, 1970) pp. 41–56, and by Robert Alter in '*Tristram Shandy* and the Game of Love', *American Scholar*, Vol. 37, (1968) pp. 316–23. One of the best essays on Sterne's stylistic idiosyncrasies is 'Sterne's Punctuation' by Roger B. Moss, in *Eighteenth Century Studies*, Vol. 15, No. 2, (Winter 1981–82) pp. 179–200, and Ian Watt examines 'The Comic Syntax of *Tristram Shandy*' in *Studies in Criticism and Aesthetics, 1660–1800: Essays in Honor of Samuel Monk Holt* (University of Minnesota Press, 1967) pp. 315–31.

## Portraits

The most famous portrait of Sterne is by Sir Joshua Reynolds (1760). A splendid bust of Sterne was made by the sculptor Joseph Nollekens in 1766, and several casts were made of it. Both these representations of Sterne can be seen at the National Portrait Gallery, London.

## Shandy Hall

Perhaps one of the pleasantest ways of learning more about Laurence Sterne is to visit his former home, Shandy Hall, at Coxwold in North Yorkshire, where he wrote most of *Tristram Shandy*. Rescued from ruin by Kenneth and Julia Monkman, it is now owned by the Laurence Sterne Trust, and houses a fine collection of Sterne memorabilia, including many beautiful editions of *Tristram Shandy*. Shandy Hall is open from June to September inclusive, on Wednesday and Sunday afternoons.

# Index

*Analysis of Beauty, The*, 51, 70
*Anatomy of Melancholy, The*, 15
*Arcadia*, 19
association of ideas, 6, 17–18

Barthes, Roland, 57, 58, 59
Beckett, Samuel, 52, 72, 75
Berenger, Richard, 54
Bradshaigh, Lady, 23
Burton, Robert, 15, 16

Cervantes, Miguel de, 11, 15
Chaucer, Geoffrey, 18
*Clarissa*, 19, 20
Coleridge, Samuel Taylor, 6

Davis, Lennard, 58
Defoe, Daniel, 18, 19, 21
Descartes, René, 11, 18
Dodsley, James, 12
Dodsley, Robert, 12
*Don Quixote*, 15
Draper, Eliza, 13

Eagleton, Terry, 72
Einstein, Albert, 80
Eliot, George, 46
*Essay Concerning Human Understanding*, 16–17

Fauconberg, Lord, 13
Fielding, Henry, 18, 21, 46, 77
Fluchère, Henri, 54
Freud, Sigmund, 80

*Gargantua*, 15
Garrick, David, 54, 55

Hall-Stevenson, John, 15

Hazlitt, William, 24, 26, 56
Hogarth, William, 13, 51, 70–1
Holtz, William V., 60, 88
Horace, 6
Hume, David, 18

Jakobson, Roman, 72
James, Henry, 77, 85
Johnson, Samuel, 18
*Joseph Andrews*, 19
*Journal to Eliza*, 13
Joyce, James, 72, 75

*Literary Theory*, 72
Locke, John, 6, 9, 11, 16–18, 49, 50, 81, 83

Mann, Thomas, 72
Meyer Spacks, Patricia, 57, 58
Meyerhoff, Hans, 82
Milton, John, 18
modernism, 72, 80, 81
*Moll Flanders*, 19
Montaigne, Michel de, 15–16
*Monthly Review, The*, 12

Nabokov, Vladimir, 72
Newton, Isaac, 11

*Pamela*, 19
*Pantagruel*, 15
Pitt, William, 13
*Political Romance, A*, 12, 15
Pope Alexander, 11
Proust, Marcel, 72, 80, 90

Rabelais, François, 11, 15, 16
realism, 19–22, 47, 76–7

Richardson, Samuel, 18, 19, 20, 21, 23, 51, 77
Robbe-Grillet, Alain, 57, 58
*Robinson Crusoe*, 19, 21

*Sentimental Journey, A*, 13, 23
Shakespeare, William, 18
Sharpe, Nathan, 10
Shklovsky, Victor, 72–5
Sidney, Philip, 19
Smollett, Tobias, 18
Sterne, Agnes, 10, 12
Sterne, Catherine, 12
Sterne, Elizabeth, 11
Sterne, Jacques, 11
Sterne, Lydia, 11
Sterne, Richard (cousin), 11

Sterne, Richard (great grandfather), 10
Sterne, Richard (uncle), 11
Sterne, Roger, 10
Swearingen, James, 86
Swift, Jonathan, 11, 15, 16, 18

*Tale of a Tub, A*, 15
Thackeray, William, 24, 26
*Time in Literature*, 82
*Tom Jones*, 19, 21

*Watt*, 52
Watt, Ian, 19, 21, 39
Woolf, Virginia, 72, 81

*York Gazetteer*, the, 12